The BounceBack

Peter Spicer

SpiceWrite Books—Waunakee, WI
ISBN: 978-0-692-14274-5
Library of Congress Control Number: (pending)
The Bounce Back | Spicer, Peter
Available Formats: eBook | Paperback distribution

Dedication

This novel is dedicated to my family, including my wife, Jessica, and son, Seton. I also want to thank my professor, Dr. Steve Sherwood, at Texas Christian University for pointing me in the right direction as I began this novel several years ago.

Chapter 1

John's eyes burned with anger, narrowing his gaze on the scuffle a few feet in front of him. He now had decisions to make, including how much he valued things like, say, his arms and legs. He could keep walking with his three basketball teammates or approach a fellow senior who had just shoved a freshman against his school locker. John hesitated, scratching his brown hair and then shoving his hands inside the pockets of his hooded sweatshirt. He took a deep breath and broke from the group, slowly making his way toward the confrontation.

John knew his six-foot-two-inch frame and thin build were no match for a guy two inches taller, with an unpleasant disposition and equal amounts of fat and muscle. He couldn't shake the inner tugging that led him to intervene and protect this student. His fought a battle between his conscience and his selfish desire to continue eating solid food the rest of the school year.

Braden Francelli, John's best friend, noticed him moving away from the herd. "John, where are you going, man?"

John ignored Braden's question and approached the student. "So what's going on, Matt? Did he not pay a bet back?"

The perpetrator was deriding the young student, who was trying to return a pair of glasses to his face. John remembered his short, thin frame bouncing off the locker a few moments ago.

Matt turned his head to glare at John. "What do you want?"

"A nice car, a good job after college, my favorite football team to win a Super Bowl, but right now I'd settle for you leaving this guy alone."

Unfortunately for John, Matt played as an offensive lineman on the football team. Punters usually didn't make good bullies, John supposed. Matt sported a crew cut and wore a brown coat and jeans suited for outdoor work. It was obvious to North High students that Matt had a short temper and got a thrill from tormenting others. People like Matt rarely picked a fight with someone their own size.

Matt continued to hold the freshman against his locker.

"Come on, Matt," John said softly. "What did he do to you?"

"I'm just messing with him," Matt replied before letting go of his victim and backing up.

John turned his attention to the freshman. "You OK?"

The student brushed a mop of dark hair off his eyebrows. He looked up at John through his small lenses and responded meekly. "Yeah."

Matt looked at the many students around him and decided the fun was over, slowly walking away while glaring at John. He stopped suddenly and took a couple steps back toward him.

"How's life on the bench?" Matt asked sarcastically before returning the scowl to his face. "This ain't over. You shouldn't have gotten into my business."

John glared at Matt, but then turned his attention to the freshman. "Come on, let's walk. Where's your next class at?"

"Math, that way," the student said, pointing.

"Alright. I'm John Zander, by the way."

"You're on the basketball team, right?"

"Yeah, I'm a senior."

The student walked into his classroom, and John retreated

the other way, back to his class on this wonderful Friday in mid-January. His teammates had scattered to their respective classes at North High, a public high school with over 1,000 students in Landover, Missouri. John slid into his seat in first-hour history next to Braden, who looked up from his phone a couple minutes before the bell rang.

Braden frowned at his friend. "Why did you have to get involved in that?"

John reacted defensively. "What was I supposed to do? That wasn't cool, and we happened to be walking by. I could have used some help from you guys."

Braden looked down at his phone, thinking for a moment. "Yeah, I don't know about that. People get pushed around all the time in the halls. You don't want to tick off our football team."

"No, of course not," John responded sarcastically. "I wouldn't want to do that. If I interrupt their off-field aggression this winter, it may affect their on-field play next fall. Seems like a logical argument."

John felt the need to justify his actions, despite Braden's discouragement. "It was the right thing to do. I think you know that. As for Matt, he'll be nothing at this time next year. He'll be lucky to find a job."

Braden looked at John, but didn't say anything, wanting to end the conversation.

Saturday night, John and Braden mingled at a well-attended school dance. Braden leaned against a wall while wearing a gray Nike sweat suit and basketball sneakers and smirked while looking at his phone. He stood a couple inches taller than John, with dark hair that covered most of his forehead but was neatly trimmed on the sides. Lanky and of Italian heritage, Braden showcased his abundant athletic ability on the basketball court.

John smirked before questioning Braden. "What's with the smirk?"

Braden continued to smile, pulling his phone out of a pocket. "I'm just trying to do the right thing, like you. I had business to attend to. Check it out, THE Stephanie Wilson. First date, tomorrow tonight, man."

John shook his head, trying to conceal a smile while shoving his hands into the pockets of his hooded sweatshirt and looking down at his jeans. Braden's success in the dating world wasn't a surprise, considering his popularity and athletic success.

"Is she here tonight?" John asked.

"Yeah, she's with her friends," Braden said with a smile. "We've been texting over the past week, but she wanted to hang out with her friends tonight."

John grinned. "She didn't want you ruining her evening?"

"No, it's not that. It would just be weird hanging out just the two of us tonight. We haven't done anything together, so we wanted a date without everyone else hanging around us."

"OK, I guess that makes sense."

John looked through the crowd of students, looking for familiar faces, as Braden sent text messages. John frowned, trying to figure out what was up with Braden lately. He had always been a pretty good friend and someone who was nice to others, but since the start of his senior year he seemed distracted and aloof. John got the impression Braden would rather hang out with the four guys starting alongside him on the basketball team rather than a scrub like him. Braden maintained good grades, better than John's in fact, but never seemed too excited about any particular subject. Academics came easy to Braden. Maybe Braden thought the NBA was in his future and did not need to work hard academically.

As teens danced in the middle of the commons, John stood

on the sidelines with Braden and glanced at a group of five senior girls chatting a few feet away. Braden looked up from his phone, catching John's gaze.

Another smirk emerged on Braden's face. "Which one? The one with the red hair?"

"Would that make me Charlie Brown?"

Braden's smirk turned into a confused look. "Who's Charlie Brown?"

"Seriously? Never mind."

"Go over there," Braden prompted. "I recognize a couple of them from our church."

"I don't know, they're all together. That's a five-on-one situation, and my odds aren't good. That's like being the only defender back and the entire offense heading your way. I don't think so."

"Dude, you've been doing this for too long. Don't you think it's time to change it up? We're almost done with school, and you've never had a single date. Oh, well, I guess you weren't meant to be a winner."

"Oh, so now I'm a loser and you're a winner because you're texting a girl?" John shot back at Braden. "Sometimes winners can become losers and losers become winners. You don't think people can change?"

"I don't know, maybe. The villain Two-Face in the Batman movie went from good to bad. It took half his face getting burned to do it, though."

"Oh, so you know about Batman but not Charlie Brown?"

John rested both hands on his jeans as if he was about to rise, thinking about proving Braden wrong. After a few seconds of thought, he stood up and walked toward the girls. Just as he approached, the group ended its conversation and two of the girls moved toward John.

John braced himself and took a deep breath. "Hi girls,

how's it going?"

The two girls, one with dark hair and the other who might have been perfect for Charlie Brown, stopped and looked with surprise at John. Courtney, the taller of the two girls who had dark hair, spoke first. "Hi."

"I never get a chance to talk to you two, and I just wanted to introduce myself."

Courtney kept the conversation going. "You're John, right?"

"Yeah, and you're Courtney and Amber?"

Courtney wore shoulder-length dark hair, while Amber's hair was red and a few inches longer than her friend's hair. Amber had a few freckles on her light skin and was a couple inches shorter than Courtney.

"Have you been at any of the basketball games lately?"

"Uh, no," Courtney responded. "Why?"

"Well, my friend Braden and I are on the team. I don't play much, though. What are you keeping busy with this year?"

"I work after school and on weekends at a fast-food restaurant," Courtney explained. "Except for tonight!"

Amber chipped in, "I'm in choir, and I don't work at a fast-food restaurant."

Courtney lightly punched Amber in the arm. "Knock it off."

"Cool," John said. "I enjoy eating fast food. That's probably more fun than making it. Well, I've gotta run, but nice talking to you. If you ever want to come out to a basketball game, I'd love to see you there."

Courtney flashed a quick smile. "Yeah, we'll see. So, are you a good dancer? Amber wants to know."

"Courtney!" Amber protested, punching her in the arm.

"I have a couple of special moves," John replied, faking seriousness. "I do the sprinkler, I can yank the mower cord, and my favorite, the robotic worm."

Courtney laughed. "Should I even ask what the heck that

is?"

"You should ask, it's a great move. I won't do it here for fear of being socially isolated after the fact, but it's a combination of the worm and the robot. It's a robot trying to do the worm after being knocked to the floor."

"It seems more like a combination of weird and stupid. A fallen robot that's still moving? You need to work on your game."

"That's what my basketball coach told me last week, sadly. I'm joking about my dance moves. I'm actually a horrible dancer, which is why I was standing over there with Braden and not getting my groove on."

"Well, we appreciate the honesty," Amber replied.

"So we go to the same church, right? Landover United Methodist?" John asked. "I've seen you both at some of the youth events."

"Yes, but now that I know you go there, maybe I'll become a Lutheran," Courtney replied.

"I think you'd be better suited for a cult or something," John said, smiling. "Anyway, on that note, I'll let you get back to all the fun. I'll catch you later."

John slowly walked away, talking to himself. "Why am I sweating profusely."

Braden smiled as John sauntered back to safety.

"I hope you got someone's number."

"Yeah right. I just introduced myself and tried not to lie about anything. I was thinking about telling them I am, in fact, a superhero."

"What's your skill, keeping a piece of lumber warm with your butt?"

"It's going to be avoiding the death penalty if you keep it up. By the way, they asked me if I was a good dancer. They set me up to fail immediately. Anyway, I'd better be heading home, my parents wanted me back before it's too late."

"Dude, it's still early. Yeah, I know. But like my parents say, nothing good happens after 5 p.m."

"You're joking, right? I've known them for a long time, and that's something they might say."

"Yeah, they actually didn't say that. They probably think that, though. They're pretty boring. My dad's favorite thing is reading the newspaper."

"What do you think they talk about with their friends?" Braden asked with a smile.

John imitated his dad's voice. "I like sweater vests, how about you? And then my mom says 'That's neat, because I love baking as much as my husband likes sweater vests!'"

Braden chuckled. "You forgot to add something about the newspaper."

John smiled. "Oh yeah, and then my dad says 'Did you read about the Chinese economy yesterday? It's so boring, which is why I love it.'"

John slid into the front seat of his Ford Focus and drove through Main Street of the 100,000-person city where plenty of store and restaurant windows adorned the street. The downtown still hummed on this Friday night. After a few turns down a quiet, residential neighborhood, John arrived at their one-level 1950's-style home as John pulled into the two-car garage next to his parents' silver Buick LeSabre. John figured the vehicle matched his parents' personalities perfectly.

John strolled in the front door of his house shortly after 9 p.m. as his parents, Rick and Betty, watched television. Rick, in his 40s, stood several inches shorter than his son, and thin remnants of dark brown hair crowned his balding head. He wore thick, dark-rimmed glasses that seemed a bit too large for his face. Betty, the same age as Rick, wore long, straight light-brown hair that grew past her shoulders.

"So, how was the dance?" Betty asked, turning away from the television.

"Good," John replied, walking down the hall to his bedroom, attempting to avoid further conversation.

John's father sat in a recliner in the living room with the newspaper next to him as he watched the television screen. Rick worked as a computer programmer, while Betty worked as a secretary. She also spent several evenings volunteering at the church, cleaning the building.

Rick looked up from his newspaper at John. "Do you have a game this week?"

"Yeah, Friday. Any chance that you'll come out to that one?"

Betty stared at her son. "John, you know I'm busy that night, and your father usually works late to finish up some work before the weekend."

"That's right," Rick agreed. "You won't be playing much anyway, right?"

John slumped his shoulders a bit and began walking toward his room. "Yeah, probably not."

After walking down a hallway along the dark carpet, John entered his room and crashed on the bed while cushioning his head on the pillow. The room's walls were white and mostly bare, adorned by a couple of small basketball posters. John often gazed out the window at his backyard from the chair at his wooden desk. A brown dresser stood next to the one closet in the room. The room was clean and neat with no clothing thrown on the floor, according to his parents' request.

These days, something other than the injustices of high school life was burning deep inside John. He knew it wasn't healthy, but he just couldn't help but water the seeds of jealousy whenever he had time to think. John grew up playing basketball with Braden and some of his classmates. He attended the same tournaments and the same practices. Now, as they reached the highest level of school sports, he had to watch Braden and others have all the fun and glory. At times, it felt like these nagging thoughts were eating him alive as each game passed. John tried hard each practice, but most of the other guards were quicker and more athletic than him. He was a better shooter than most guys, but he rarely had the opportunity in practice to showcase that ability.

Monday morning, John threw on some jeans and a hooded sweatshirt and wandered out to the kitchen table to grab some cereal before heading off to classes. His mom stood at the counter setting the table.

"Remember, you have the college visit at State University tomorrow, OK?" Betty reminded John politely Monday morning. "Hopefully, your application will impress them."

"Well, I'm not impressed by it, so why should they be?" John muttered between bites of cereal.

"Just what I want to do," he thought. "Visit a college and tell everyone I have no idea why I should be there."

A short time later, John's car wheeled into the school parking lot as students poured across the lot, heading into the large, recently-built new building. Once inside, John worked the lock on his locker as Braden leaned against his own locker just a few feet away.

"Hey, I'm heading over there to talk to Stephanie and her friends," Braden said. "Come on over, and I'll introduce you."

John kept staring into his locker. "Yeah, just let me grab my books."

The two seniors trudged over to a group of five girls forming a semi-circle around their lockers, talking. Each stood there, phone in hand chatting loudly. Braden worked his way in between Stephanie and one of her friends and greeted

10

everyone. Braden began talking as John stood just outside the group sheepishly while he watched his friend attentively listen to everything Stephanie said. She had shoulder-length blonde hair with a deep tan and wore a dance team shirt.

"Everyone, this is John," announced Braden. "He's on the team with me. We've been playing basketball together since grade school. He attends dances and basketball games, yet doesn't actually participate in either activity. He's a master observer."

"Cool," one of the girls stated with a smirk while the others giggled. Stephanie nodded in his direction while texting someone.

John waved to the group. "Sadly, that's all true."

"Well, this is awkward," John thought to himself after realizing no one responded to his comment.

John watched the group share gossip while looking at their phones.

"Stephanie, you coming over after practice tonight?" Braden asked.

"I've got homework I gotta get done."

"Come on, you can put it off."

"Until when? It's due in the morning and I don't have any other time. We'll do something this weekend like I told you."

As the bell rang, John tagged along with Braden to class.

"Dude, you guys are fighting already?"

"Shut up."

"Go easy on her man, if she's got homework, she's got homework."

"Why don't you mind your own business?"

"Fine, but I'll remind you that the next time you bug me about approaching women."

The two plopped into their seats at the first-hour history class they shared.

"John, you better be getting me the ball in practice tonight."

"Why?"

"I've been on fire this week, I've been hitting everything."

"How about you just let me do what's best for the team?"

"Getting me the ball is what's best for the team."

John laughed, shaking his head while hoping Braden didn't actually believe what he said.

During the lunch hour, John stopped by Mr. Harmon's classroom. Don and his wife, Julie, attended John's church. The Harmons had been friends with John's family for many years. Don taught history, and John took several classes from him during his high-school career. Don stood at the same height as John and wore neatly combed brown hair and clean attire with a black sweater over a button-down shirt and dress pants. The Harmons had a 10-year-old son and an eight-year-old daughter. John respected Don and Julie, both in their early 40s, because of their friendliness and how they treated others.

Don "Hey John, how about that football game the other night?"

"Yeah, that was fun to watch," John replied.

"We're coming out to your big game Friday night," Don added. "You guys are gonna get it done against West High, right?

"I'm sure Braden and the guys will give it their best," John said quietly.

"Aren't you going to be knocking down the big shots?"

John responded with a touch of bitterness in his voice. "I'm probably going to be keeping my seat on the bench warm like usual."

Shortly after the school day ended, John walked into the gym dressed for practice as the sound of basketball sneakers already filled the large gym. Coach Doug Thompson, a tall man who carried extra weight, paced the floor with a whistle around his neck. John thought he was an alright guy but fiery. He worked the players hard but wasn't overbearing. John worked on his free throws and three-pointers as players filed into the gym. He was part of a 13-man roster and one of five seniors. Braden worked on a few of his post moves underneath the basket.

Braden looked in John's direction as one of his shots banked in. "I'm gonna be doing this all night. Are you planning on just shooting threes in the next game?"

John responded, quoting a former NBA player. "You know I have to take threes, because there aren't any fours."

Senior forward DaVonte Keys dribbled past John and into the lane before lazily throwing up a floater. "I've seen your vertical, so that's a good plan."

Coach Thompson's whistle blasted, and everyone jogged over to him at center court as he addressed the group. "OK, listen up. You guys know what a big game this is Friday against West High. We need a sharp practice tonight. We're going to go over our defense and make sure everyone is on the same page. We can't give up easy shots and have to make them work for everything they get. After our drills, I want the starting lineup out on the court with everyone else on the side."

The team dribbled through cones and worked on other ball handling drills before the starters made their way onto the court to work on defense. Braden and DaVonte joined fellow starters Teyshaun White, Joe Anthony and Rashad Alexander on the court. Joe, a 6'4" forward, was the only junior in the starting lineup. John wiped sweat from the hair over his forehead as he stood by fellow senior Darnell Jackson, a backup point guard who got plenty of minutes each game. Next to them stood a group of six juniors. The team was a diverse bunch, with John and Braden the only two white seniors on the team. Juan Hernandez, a speedy junior guard, was the lone Hispanic player on the team. Terrance White, another junior guard, was the only player who had a sibling on the team. Sam Stevens, Erick Samuels, and Dan Zimmerman spent a lot of time hanging out together since they were all junior forwards. Dominique Carter, a junior guard, rounded out the team.

Sam Stevens, one of the junior forwards, continued his role as team jokester. "Remember, we gotta look good tomorrow night, so I was thinking tearaway tuxedos. How about that?"

John flashed a smile in the direction of the goofy-looking guy with moppy blonde hair falling in his eyes. Sam's jokes helped bring the bench guys together. Everyone laughed just looking at him. Sam was tall, about 6'3", and quite pudgy.

"You do that, and coach will make you the water boy," Erick responded.

"But isn't that your job?" Sam continued. "You're not on this team because of your game. I take you to school every practice."

John tuned out the chatter and thought about wasting his time with a college visit.

"I hope the school doesn't ask why they should admit me," John thought to himself. "To get out of my parents' house probably isn't the best answer."

John still thought State was his best option, though. He was getting out of class tomorrow, so it couldn't be too bad. His parents took half a day off from work to visit the campus with him. John's attention turned back to basketball.

"Alright, I want the second-string offense out here," Coach Thompson barked, whistle around the neck of his sweat-soaked t-shirt. His wind pants made a swooshing noise with each step. The offense passed the ball around, forcing the zone defense to rotate. John, stationed on one of the wings, found

14

himself alone with the ball after a pass. He instinctively fired up a three ball, which swooshed through the net.

"John!" Coach Thompson screamed. "This is a drill. I want the defense to work. This isn't shootaround! Go again."

John cocked his head, giving coach a look that said, "You've got to be kidding me."

"Come on, John," Braden scolded, giving him an exasperated look.

John whipped the ball back to the point guard, churning with anger. He held his emotions back, knowing if he let the coach know what he really thought, he would be running sprints for the rest of his life. If he let Braden and company know how he felt, he would need to make new friends. He had a feeling that joining the Chess Club for lunch each day might not be his style, so he needed to bottle everything up one more time.

Friday evening, John sat quietly on the locker room bench before the game. Teammates gathered around him dribbling basketballs as they sat, headphones covering their ears. John thought about his college visit a few days ago that included a tour of the tall, plain buildings that adorned the campus. He didn't feel comfortable on the campus. Coach walked quickly into the room, clapping his hands.

Players stood, gathering around him as he addressed the team. "Be the tougher team tonight. Let's execute and show them what Leopard basketball is all about, alright? Let's break it down. Execute... on three."

The players broke the huddle and lined up at the entrance of the locker room, ready to sprint into the gym for layups. Braden walked over to John, giving him a fist pump.

"Let's get it done," John encouraged half-heartedly.

The PA announcer's voice boomed throughout the gym. "Ladies and gentlemen, please welcome your North High

Leopards."

Players ran onto the court as the packed group of fans in the bleachers roared. John found a place in the layup line and glanced up to find Don and Julie in the crowded stands. They had big smiles on their faces as they sat at the top of the bleachers. It was a full house, which included a good group of fans from West High. After the starting lineups, John and his fellow reserves made their way to the bench.

"Gentlemen of the board," Sam bellowed as everyone began to sit. "Let us now begin this meeting."

John sat in the center of the group and watched his teammates out on the court. He looked over at Dominique Carter, a backup junior guard, trying to find someone to talk to. "Man, I was really hoping I could get a few minutes each game, you know? At least you have next year."

Dominique kept watching the game with a disinterested expression on his face. "Well, you never know when they're going to need a three-point shooter. You got the shot."

The mood at the end of the bench was a bit lighter, as Erick Samuels, a junior forward, voiced a complaint. "Hey, come on, give me some room, Sam, you've got nothing but empty bench next to you and aren't giving me one inch of space."

John glanced around the gym, looking for people he recognized, such as Courtney and Amber, but no such luck. His good friend Matt, the bully, was among the crowded student section, thankfully not near any freshmen. John tried to refocus on the game, as Braden knocked in a couple jumpers, but his thoughts strayed to the last practice where coach exploded at him. The incident just added to John's growing list of burdens, such as deciding what to do with his boring life, maintaining his friendships and not letting his inner frustrations out of their cage. He felt like he could lose his grip on those at any point.

The team played well, as Braden poured in 16 points that night, including two three-pointers. After a tied score through three quarters, North began pulling away and had a 10-point lead over West as the final minute approached. John looked up at the scoreboard as the time ticked away. Coach Thompson waved John and four junior reserves over to the scorer's table with little over 30 seconds to go, but after a few fast breaks the clock read zeroes. John slowly rose from his seat on the floor.

"So close, yet so far," Sam concluded humorously as a teammate tried to help him up.

John wanted to remain on the floor in disgust and maybe have a minor meltdown, but he slowly rose and joined his teammates. He congratulated Braden, as Don and Julie walked up behind them. Don and Julie wore North High jackets with their jeans. Julie, who wore her dark hair in a ponytail, smiled at John and Braden while standing close to her husband. They left their children with a babysitter this night, enjoying a few hours off from parenting.

Don smiled at Braden, while shaking John's hand. "Hey, how are the victors?"

"Braden, you played an incredible game," Julie exclaimed.

Braden walked toward the group of girls headed his way. "Thanks Mrs. Harmon, I'll see you guys later."

Braden paused momentarily, turning to John. "Hey, come over Saturday morning, OK?"

"Yeah, I'll be there."

Unaware of John's inner turmoil, Don joked about John's lack of playing time. "You looked good at the scorer's table."

John held back what he wanted to get off his chest but was afraid of the consequences. John said his goodbyes and followed the sound of rap music back to the locker room, his white jersey with gold and blue trim untucked. John sat down, not sure why he didn't happy about the win. He knew he should feel good, but what could he do? A bunch of the guys drove to a restaurant after the game, but John showered and headed for the exit.

"Where are you going, John?" Braden asked John as he pushed the locker room door open.

"Home."

"We're going to a restaurant."

"Well, I'm not."

"You're turning into a loser man, we just won the game."

John stared at him "I'm a loser, huh?"

"Maybe you're not hungry because you didn't burn enough calories tonight."

"Wow, thanks."

With that, John retreated to his car in the now nearly empty parking lot. Once behind the wheel, John drove silently home, realizing the year was slipping away from him, and he wasn't able to do anything about it.

The next morning, John drove past the school and turned into a subdivision of large homes, all built within the last few years. He wound his way past one large two-story after another before pulling into the driveway of Braden's white, two-floor home with a three-car garage. He pulled his vehicle next to the outdoor basketball hoop and headed for the front door.

Braden's mom, Cheryl, greeted him, wearing workout attire and holding a bottle of water. "Hi John, come on in, Braden's downstairs. You guys played great last night." "Yeah, it was a good win," John said. "Braden played well. So where's Brandon?"

"Oh, he has a hockey tournament out of town today with his seventh-grade team," Cheryl explained, discussing her other son. "We're heading up there this afternoon to see him."

John made his way down the carpeted stairway and into the finished recreation room, where Braden was slouched on a long, wrap-around couch that faced a large, flat screen television. Through the doorway was a workout room where Braden's mom began running on a treadmill.

"Hey, you up for some air hockey?" Braden asked.

"Of course, why do you think I come over here?" John joked. "If I wanted to be at a boring house, I'd stay home."

The two began launching the puck at each other's goal. A billiards table stood behind them. Foosball and ping pong tables filled out the room, which also featured a bar area.

"Well, I made it to the scorer's table," John stated halfway through their game.

Braden didn't respond, concentrating on the game at hand. He rocketed the puck off the side of the table and into the goal. "Game."

"This just wasn't the senior season I had hoped for," John continued introspectively.

"So what? We're winning."

"Yeah, that's great, but I just wish I could, you know, be part of it."

Braden responded flippantly. "It's a long season, maybe coach'll work you in."

"I think that might be wishful thinking. It's already late January, and the regular season will be over in a month."

"Well, that's the way it goes."

"That's easy for you to say, isn't it? You're lighting it up in games, and I'm not even allowed to shoot in practice."

Braden stared at him blankly, looking surprised by this admission.

John changed the subject before he could say something he might regret. He was a guest, after all, so he decided not to push his luck. "So what are you and Stephanie doing

19

tonight?"

Braden flipped through channels on the television. "I think we might be doing dinner and a movie."

"Ah yes, the old dinner and a movie," John joked. "It's a dating classic. So what do you know about Stephanie other than she's on the dance team?"

"Uhhh...I think her parents are getting a divorce or something. The father's gone on business a lot, and her parents aren't getting along."

"How's Stephanie taking it?" John enquired.

"She's fine, things haven't been that great at home for quite a while."

"Do you have anything in common with her?"

"Not really, but she's hot, and that's the most important thing!"

Braden pointed to the television set.

"Alright, the football playoff game's on. You think these guys have a chance to win?"

Sunday afternoon, John sat on the couch watching television and decided to give Braden a call.

"How was last night?" John asked.

A smile broke across Braden's face. "Players gonna play."

"I'm pretty sure I've never been able to say that."

"That's probably true."

"Hey, so what movie did you see last night?

"I don't want to discuss details!"

"OK, what are you hiding?" John said. "What was it? I just want the name of the movie."

Braden hesitated before answering. "Umm, I think it was called Wedding Day."

John cracked up. "Nice. Sorry I missed out on that."

A few minutes later, Don Harmon called John on the family's landline.

"So, how about championship Sunday you come over and watch one of the football games at our place?" Don asked. "You OK with pizza?"

John grinned, ready with a reply. "I think I'll be OK with that."

John could tell his parents he was watching curling, and they wouldn't know the difference.

After basketball practice Monday, John returned home and walked through the kitchen trying to determine whether he should be scared of what was coming his way for dinner or be pleasantly surprised. Nothing too healthy, he hoped.

"John, you have something in the mail from State University," his mother said, opening the oven.

John looked on the counter at the official-looking envelope and slowly opened it. He silently read it before dropping the envelope to the ground and leaning against the counter, not sure how to feel about what he just read.

Chapter 2

John stepped on the letter while walking through the living room and grabbed a seat at the kitchen table with a blank stare on his face.

John's mother looked at him with a baffled expression. "What?"

"I didn't get in."

"How could that be? Your grades are good, you're on the basketball team, you have a job in the summer. Your letters of recommendation were wonderful."

"My ACT score could have been higher, I guess, and my grades are good but not spectacular" John muttered. "I thought for sure you'd get in. They must have a lot of applicants."

John pulled himself up and walked into the living room, where he plopped down on the couch, staring at the television screen. "Well, check that off as one of my options," John thought. "I guess that narrows it down to either Harvard or Yale."

At the dinner table that night, John's dad tried to convince him that many other state schools might take him, but John realized should plan to travel further from home to attend school. He wouldn't be headed to the same school as Braden, who might play lower-level NCAA Division-1 basketball. Although John finished his dinner, he walked back to his room with an empty feeling in his stomach. John didn't have a good feeling about the coming week.

Tuesday morning, John opened his locker as Braden made his way over. John wanted to immediately get the bad news off his chest. "I didn't get into State."

Braden looked at John while leaning against a locker. "Not a big deal, there are plenty of schools around. It just means you won't be going to the schools I apply for."

"Great, thanks."

"Well, cheer up. Why don't you chat with Stephanie's friends over there with me?"

Braden walked toward the group of girls, all standing in their usual semi-circle by the lockers. John took his awkward place just behind the gathering, while Braden mingled. John didn't say a word, and he noticed Braden looking at him with a frown.

The bell mercifully rang a few minutes later, as John and Braden walked to first-hour history class while Braden questioned John. "Come on, man, you don't seem too excited about hanging out with us. What? Don't you like my new friends?"

John hesitated before attempting to explain a complex issue. "They just look at their phones and gossip. How am I supposed to get excited about that and join in? I just don't have anything in common with any of them. And they don't seem that nice, either."

Braden glared back at John. "What do you mean? You don't like Stephanie, either?"

"I don't know. I don't know her at all, and I'm just a third wheel around you two."

"Maybe you're just jealous."

"Yes, I would just love it if I could hang out with that group of girls all the time. My life would be so much cooler. And who cares if the girl they're ripping doesn't have perfect fashion sense?"

"I'm dating Stephanie, not her friends."

"But doesn't it bother her that they're bashing others for stupid reasons?"

"You think too much, you've just got to let it go."

"What does that even mean?"

Braden and John sat down in the classroom as John continued the conversation. "Look, I don't know Stephanie, and I'm not judging her, but the whole group seems superficial. And why do you care if I like them? That's one of the last places I'd go looking for friends."

The bell rang, as Mr. Jones began his lecture. Braden leaned over his desk, continuing the conversation with John. "I'm just trying to do you a favor, John, introducing you to friends. If you don't want to mingle, and only want to hang out with losers, go for it."

The middle-aged teacher, wearing a dress shirt and tie, stopped mid-sentence peering at the two conversationalists through the bottom of his bifocal glasses. "Mr. Zander and Mr. Francilli."

A few students attempted to stifle laughs as Mr. Jones continued. "Is there something important that needs to be discussed with the class?"

Braden, whose face turned a bit red, attempted to humor Mr. Jones. "Well, actually, my pal John and I were just having a difference in opinion about some of my good friends. You see, young John here doesn't understand..."

Mr. Jones cut him off. "That will be enough, unless you'd like to explain it after class or in a 10-page paper."

Braden smirked, quietly responding, "That's OK. It wasn't that important."

As the bell finally rang at the end of first hour, John rose from his desk and continued his conversation with Braden. "It just seems that Stephanie's group is all about popularity and not that concerned with being nice to others."

Braden frowned, with a confused look. "It's not her fault she's loved by everyone."

"Yeah, but it is her fault if she's in petty social media fights and looks down on those not in their circle of friends."

"You think she's shallow?"

"I'm not saying that, I don't know her. But I do know they aren't interested in making new friends and all they talk about is pointless stuff."

Braden frowned. "The future, huh? You don't even know where the heck you're going to college or what you want to major in next year, and you're going to tell me about the future? Why don't you get back to me on that one, huh?"

At that moment, Stephanie walked up to Braden in the hallway. She hesitated, frowning slightly, as if she sensed the two young men were having an unpleasant conversation. "Everything good?"

Braden looked at Stephanie and then glared back at John. "Yeah, everything is good just as it is."

John leaned against his locker, while his eyes glazed over watching Braden and Stephanie go their way. He shook his head, talking to himself. "Great, now what?"

Just as John walked to class, Matt and a few of his offensive lineman friends approached him. Matt wore a sinister grin on his face. "Hey, John, just wanted to introduce a few friends of mine. I told them all about you."

John decided to stand up to them. "Hey, weren't you the guys I saw in that all-you-can -eat buffet commercial the other night? Or was I thinking of a children's arcade ad? Maybe it was both."

The group didn't respond, and a serious look came over John's face. "Look, I don't have time for your garbage, Matt, and excuse me for asking you to stop picking on a freshman half your size."

John looked at the three students with him and wondered how they could support this jerk. "Are you guys okay with him pushing around a freshman just so he can feel better about himself?"

"Shut up!" Matt snapped. "My boys here just wanted to let you know who's going to be hurting you the next time you decide to bother me."

"Yeah, well, if I see you picking on someone, I'll be talking to you once again."

The warning bell rang, and Matt decided to get going. "We'll just see how that goes for you then, huh?"

John noticed his hands shaking as he walked to class. Maybe leaving town next fall for college wouldn't be so difficult after all.

The Leopards went on the road that night to play Kennedy High, one of the teams in the bottom half of the conference, and everyone on the North High team licked their chops, looking forward to a dominating win. John sat alongside junior reserve guard Dominique Carter on the bench as the game began. Dominique was about 5'10 with a small afro, giving him a couple additional inches of height. Dominique usually came off the bench at the same time as John at the end of lopsided games. He possessed quickness but struggled with shooting and committing turnovers, keeping him on the bench.

North High jumped out to a 10-0 lead, and Dominique began rubbing his hands together while looking over at John. "This is the game I get some action. Did you know I haven't scored a point all season? That's gonna end tonight."

John could see the excitement on Dominique's face and couldn't help but feel the same way. He usually tried to suppress those feelings more than his younger teammates. He didn't think much about the game, considering the other issues on his mind. Braden hadn't said much to him since the incident earlier that day, and he worried their friendship could soon end. John figured Braden might ditch him to hang out exclusively with his fellow starters. Even on a racially diverse team like North, friendship circles formed based on age and playing time. Benchwarmers mingled with benchwarmers and starters with starters.

With just over three minutes left in the game, the Leopards held a 70-43 lead, and Coach Thompson waved over the handful of benchwarmers. Juan Hernandez, the backup junior point guard, ran the offense for the reserve group, and John played shooting guard. With inexperienced players on the floor, the game pace was frenetic – lots of fast breaks and turnovers.

Less than two minutes remained in the game, and Juan dished the ball to John on the left wing. Ten feet separated John and the defender, but as he rose in his shooting motion John saw Dominique to his left, open in the corner behind the three-point arc. He hesitated a split second before firing a pass Dominique's way. Dominique fired a shot, and the ball swished through the net to extend North's lead by three more points. The Leopards fans who made the trip cheered loudly, chanting Dominique Carter's last name. He ran down the court with a huge smile on his face, pointing at the crowd.

By the end of the game, all four of John's court mates finished the game with points, giving the Leopards an 82-50 win. Everyone on the team entered the locker room wearing smiles. John thought about his performance as he tossed his basketball uniform on the floor. He did not turn the ball over during his time on the court and kept the offense going, but team play left him scoreless. He pondered whether he should have tried to put some points on the board and whether coach noticed his efforts.

Braden walked by John on his way to the shower. "You had a wide open shot there, John, and you passed it. That was your chance, so don't wonder why you're not playing. You've got to show something if you want to play."

John glared at Braden. "Dominique hadn't scored all season, and he was wide open."

"So were you. Sometimes you have to take what's yours."

"Yeah, well, I'm not you."

John stared out the bus window on the ride home as players celebrated and goofed around. He figured tonight may be the most playing time he sees all season, and if he didn't impress the coaches, he may not get another chance.

The following morning before school, John stopped by Don Harmon's classroom to say hello. Don worked at his desk, finalizing the morning's lesson as John strolled in.

"Hey John, good win last night."

"Yeah, everyone played well."

"How'd you do?"

"Not well, I was the only guy to not score."

"Not a big deal, at least you played, right?"

"Yeah. I feel terrible about it though, 'cause I didn't do anything to impress coach."

"Just keep working, I guess."

John put his head down. "I'll see ya."

"Hey John, is everything OK?"

"Yeah, never been better."

"You sure?"

"Of course."

After eating lunch with some of his teammates a couple hours later, John walked down the hall, passing Courtney and Amber.

"Don't I know you from somewhere?" John joked.

"Yeah, we were on that TV show," Courtney said.

"Cheaters or the Bachelorette?"

"Very funny!"

John turned to Amber. "So, what's the next big event for your choir?"

Amber brushed her curly red hair off her shoulder, responding quietly. "Um, I think we have a spring concert in May, but that's a long way off. I'm singing in a group for the solo and ensemble contest this spring."

"Cool, that's exciting. I don't think I could handle the pressure of performing in front of people."

"That probably rules out one of your career choices, the circus, right?" Courtney added. "And that probably explains why you're on the bench in basketball.

"Hilarious!"

Amber looked over at Courtney. "Be nice!"

John looked back at Amber. "I was going to say - before Courtney explained what a failure I am - that I'm sure you'll do well."

"Thanks," Amber said quietly, brushing her hair behind her ear.

As they chatted by a row of lockers, John noticed the freshman Steve sitting on the floor with his back against a locker and his head down just behind where the two girls stood.

John walked over to where Steve sat. "Hey, I remember you from the other day. Are you OK?"

The student looked up, blinking. After a few moments of silence, Steve looked up at John "My grandpa has been in the hospital all week and probably won't make it."

John's mouth opened, searching for words. "Steve, I'm sorry. Is there anything I can do?"

Steve shook his head.

"Well I'll be thinking of you, man. If you need anyone to talk to, just let me know."

The two girls stood quietly, not sure if they should say anything.

John turned to Courtney and Amber. "Well, hey, I really enjoyed talking to you. Except for everything Courtney said about me. I hope you have a great day, and best of luck this week with school and everything."

"Yeah, thanks," Courtney responded.

"And Amber, keep Courtney from drinking the hate-orade."

"What is hate-orade?" Amber asked.

"It a delicious beverage Courtney makes by mixing a powdery mixture of hate into a sugary energy drink. She has some each morning so she doesn't run out of meanness."

"Wow, that's funny. I'll try to keep her from being too mean to people."

As John made his way to class, Don Harmon passed him in the hall. "You're still coming over to our house for the game this Sunday, right?"

"Yeah, I'll be there."

Don looked past John with a questioning look. "I usually see Braden with you, where is he?"

"I saw him in classes today, but he usually sits with his fellow starters at lunch. Scrubs like me sit elsewhere. He's the big starter now."

"Well, say hello to him for me. I hope you guys stay friends."

After practice that evening, John sat at the desk in his room, trying to concentrate on homework, but couldn't focus. He thought about the freshman he met, the girls he talked with, and his performance at practice. He eventually finished his homework and rolled into bed later than he wanted.

The next morning, John walked down the freshman hallway on the way to class and noticed Steve standing at his locker. He nodded at John, who stopped to greet him.

"Hey Steve, I've been thinking about you, man. You hanging in there?"

"Yeah, thanks for asking."

A few moments later, John walked into history class and slid into his seat next to Braden.

John looked over at him, trying to read his mood. "So, what did you do last night?"

Braden looked up from his notebook. "What do you mean?"

"Did you finish your homework."

"Actually, Stephanie finished it for me. I hung out with her last night, and we ended up watching TV for too long. She's better at history than me, so I just had her do most of it."

"How impressive. Since you're having other people do stuff for you, mind if I take your minutes on the court. I'm better at it than you, so you might as well let me do that for you."

"Nah, I'll hold onto them for now."

After lunch that day, John wandered into Don Harmon's classroom. Don sat at his desk eating lunch and summoned John over.

"Have a seat, man. What are you up to?"

"Not much. I just wanted to ask some college advice."

"Really? You applied to State, right?"

"Yeah, I didn't get in, so now I'm looking for another option."

"So what are you looking for in a college? Any specific criteria?"

"A school with a cool nickname is great for starters. Just kidding. I haven't really thought about it much."

"Well, if you don't have a major in mind, that's OK. Do you want to be close to home or doesn't that matter?"

31

"I'd like to go somewhere in the state, and somewhere not too big I guess. That's about it."

"Well, maybe you can look at some of the smaller state schools. But if you want to go somewhere next fall, you should probably start filling out applications right away."

"Well, how did you decide?"

"I knew I wanted to teach, so I went to State, which had a good program."

"Yeah, so it seems you knew what you were doing."

"Yes, but lots of students don't know. You'll figure it out, there's nothing to worry about."

"I worry about it all the time, though. I'm afraid of making a mistake and trying to major in something I won't like or don't do well."

"Look, you have time to figure all that out. I don't know if you know this or not, but a lot of adults switch careers, and that happens all the time. Some people are forced to do something else and others just don't like what they're doing and want to make a switch. College is more than just job training, you know. You take classes that help you learn more about different subjects and help you become a better citizen and well-informed person."

"Yeah, that's a good point," said John as he got up from the desk he sat in. "Thanks for the advice."

"Yeah, anytime. Are you doing OK?"

"I'm just not enjoying anything right now. Basketball isn't fun, and nothing else is, either."

"Well, you should try to, it's your senior year."

"I'll keep that in mind."

That evening, the Leopards held a final practice before Friday night's game against South High, a team with a .500 record on the season. John once again played the part of the pawn, helping the starters solidify their game plan against a scout team.

John overheard Dominique bragging about his three-point shot from the previous game as players watched the starting group run plays.

"I got game, coach just needs to put me in, and he'll see me put up mad points all night long," Dominique told his teammates.

John thought about how he passed up his own shot to get Dominique involved.

"I heard two girls asked you out after the game?" Sam asked.

"It was more like three, but that's OK," Dominique added. "The ladies like the three-ball."

"Dude, you made one shot!" John exclaimed. "Get a grip, man."

"That's one more than you've made," Dominique shot back.

"You're kidding, right?" John asked. "I did pass you the ball."

"Some of us just perform when the lights go on."

John shook his head.

The final 30 minutes of practice, the backups scrimmaged the starters, which John enjoyed. John's idea of a good time evaporated quickly when Braden and the starters fared well against his group. John could only watch as his teammates fumbled the ball around, turning it over frequently.

Braden walked by John during a stop in the action and smirked at him. "Why don't you just save some time and hand me the ball. We're going to take it from one of your teammates, so let us conserve our energy."

John glared at Braden. "Keep talking."

"I will, we've already dominated you punks."

Coach Thompson's booming voice grabbed the attention of the players as practice neared its end. "OK, last possession, right here."

Juan, the backup point guard, dribbled past half court and attempted to pass it to John at one of the wings near the three-point line. Braden, on defense, read the pass and stepped in front of it. John watched him grab the ball before it reached his hands, and Braden quickly dribbled down the court. Frustrated, John chased after him despite knowing this was the last play. Braden slowed down as he reached the hoop, assuming no one was anywhere near him. John caught up just as Braden left his feet to put the shot off the backboard. John jumped as high as he could and crashed into Braden, who landed hard on the floor.

Braden grabbed his neck but quickly rose to his feet, looking for John, who landed on his side. John stood, uninjured, but Braden returned John to the floor with one hard push. "What the heck, man? What are you doing?"

John picked himself up quickly and, without saying a word, threw a punch that brushed Braden's jaw. Braden grabbed John, pushing him against the padded back wall of the gym, while John fought back.

Coach Thompson's voice ended the scuffle. "That's enough! John, you're done. Get out of here! Consider yourself off the team. I won't tolerate fighting."

John glared at Coach Thompson, ready to take him on next. "Yeah, well I've had enough of your practices. The only people they help are prima donnas like Braden here, who's a first-class jerk. You don't care about that, do you though? As long as the team's winning, you don't care how he treats me! Your practices don't benefit anyone but the five guys starting, so I've got nothing to lose!"

John picked up the basketball and threw it at Braden's knees while heading for the exit. Braden looked stunned at this turn of events.

Coach Thompson, whose face turned red, took a couple steps toward John and screamed at the top of his lungs. "Get out!"

Chapter 3

The gym fell quiet until the sound of a punch colliding with a locker outside the gym broke the silence. John trudged off to the locker room, ignoring the pain from his now throbbing fist that reminded of the mess he created. He felt Braden's attitude pushed him to a boiling point. John sat alone on a bench in the empty locker room, thinking about what happened. He knew he ruined his reputation with Braden and his teammates. John couldn't believe in one practice he lost his spot on the team, and no doubt his teammates would soon spread details of the incident throughout the school. John wondered how much flights to another country might cost.

John quickly dressed and got out of the locker room before practice ended. He dreaded his return home, where he looked forward to facing his parents, whom he felt knew nothing of his inner frustrations. John hoped the car ride would last forever, but it didn't, and he eventually made his way through the front door.

John's mother greeted him from the kitchen, where she pushed a casserole into the oven. "Hi John, how was school and basketball practice?"

"Um, we're going to have to talk. I need to shower, so I'll wait until dinner."

Betty gave John a blank expression as he walked by her and Rick, who sat in the living room watching the news on television.

John showered and made the trip to the dining room table, where he knew it might be one of the worst family meals ever.

At least it wouldn't be dull, he figured. John pulled up a chair as Rick and Betty waited. John's mother wore a nervous look on her face as the family prayed before the dinner.

Betty spoke timidly while looking across the table at John. "So, what's going on, John?"

John looked at his mother and then back at his father, waiting a few seconds before answering. "Um, I got kicked off the basketball team."

John's admission caused silence at the Zander family dinner table.

After what John felt like was an eternity, Rick spoke first. "How did that happen, John?"

John felt a lump in his throat. "I got mad at Braden and punched him."

Betty looked at her son with her mouth open. "Why would you do that? And why Braden?"

"He's been a jerk this year, and I was tired of him pushing me around. He always had some demeaning little comment for me. Nothing has gone right this year, and he was sticking it to me that I wasn't playing. And the backups I have to play with are selfish and don't have much talent. So, that's that."

John's father shook his head and put down his napkin. "What is wrong with you? This isn't how we raised you, John. You should know better than this."

John glared at his father. "Thanks for understanding. You think this is what I wanted to do? It just happened after everything boiled over. You think I like sitting on the bench and taking Braden's garbage?"

A frown crossed Rick's face. "John, your mother and I didn't play sports, and it looks like you shouldn't be playing them. Sports are unimportant, so for you to go off and get in so much trouble over a game is unacceptable. I guess we shouldn't have let you play if this is what was going to happen."

John fired back. "Just because basketball doesn't mean anything to you doesn't mean it shouldn't matter to me. I wanted to do well this year, and you have no idea how much this year has stunk."

John's mother finally spoke; "John, I don't know what to say. You've never had these kinds of problems before and now this?"

John rose from the table, ready to escape the conversation. "I don't want to talk about this anymore. I just want to crash and deal with this mess tomorrow."

Betty tried to coax him back. "John, you need to finish your dinner."

"I can't. I'm not hungry, I feel sick to my stomach and I'm getting out of here."

John trudged off to his room while his parents remained silent for the moment. John landed face down on his bed, wondering how to survive the next day and what might be in store for him. At least he only had to make it through one more day before the weekend.

John headed to his locker the next morning, as a group of senior guys, whom he didn't know, made their way to him through the crowded hall.

One of the guys in the group, who wore a big smile, questioned John. "Hey John, is it true Braden put you on your butt yesterday?"

John looked over at the guys with indifference. "Guys, do me a favor and get lost, OK?"

One of the other guys in the group kept at him. "We're just telling you what your teammates said, man. You're off the team now, right?"

"Why do you guys care? One less guy on the bench shouldn't make a difference to you fans, right?"

"No, we just want to hear some details about the fight. We haven't heard about anything this exciting in a while. You should contact the school newspaper with your story. People would love to read about Braden dropping you."

John slammed his locker and forced his way through the group of guys. "It's been a real pleasure. Go bother someone who actually thinks you're funny."

John shook his head as he made his way through the hall. He passed teammates Sam Stevens, Erick Samuels, Dan Zimmerman and Dominique Carter, who all stood in the middle of the hall chatting. As John passed, the group all turned to look at him, as if expecting him to say something.

John felt embarrassed but muttered a greeting. "Hey guys, how's it going?"

Sam, always the outgoing one, responded. "Hey, it's the fighter."

Sam began throwing punches in the air, as his teammates laughed. "He throws a right and then a left, but wait, ref Thompson is calling the fight. It's over. Braden retains the heavyweight title!"

John stopped to look at them and just shook his head while walking to class.

At lunch, John looked for someone to sit with but couldn't find an empty seat next to anyone he felt comfortable around. He retreated to the back of the commons, where he sat by himself. While eating, John looked over at the table next to him, where a group of senior girls chatted noisily. One of the girls looked John's way while whispering something into her friend's ear.

One of the girls finally said something to John. "Hey, so are you the guy who got in the fight last night?"

John gave them a frustrated look. "Yeah, I'm the guy. Would you like my autograph?"

The girls just giggled and then returned to talking amongst themselves. John looked over at a table of senior basketball players, and he remembered the team had a game that night. John felt the knot in his stomach tighten, realizing he'd miss it. He couldn't undo anything and felt hopeless.

As John left his locker at the end of the day, two of his now former teammates, Teyshaun White and Rashad Alexander, nearly bumped into him. Teyshaun and Rashad, both senior starting guards, stopped and gave John an angry look while shaking their heads.

Teyshaun spoke first. "Nice work yesterday, John. Getting kicked off the team, fighting with your coach and teammate, and ticking everybody off all in one night's work. You're one special dude. Have fun sitting on your butt while we go all the way to state. Maybe you can get tickets."

Rashad pointed at John while laughing at his friend's comments. The remarks caught John off guard, and he couldn't decide whether to fire back or try to apologize for the manner in which he had conducted himself.

John glared at the two of them as he walked toward the door. "Whatever."

John sat alone Friday night and all day Saturday, thinking about what happened. Saturday afternoon, John watched football and basketball on television in the living room, while his parents shopped. He tried not to think about the road win against Lincoln he missed Friday night or that his playing days were over after all these years of basketball. Maybe he could play intramural basketball next year at college, but it wouldn't be the same as the tough competition and loud crowds high-school basketball provided. Just getting through the last few months of school could be tough, considering he had now alienated his best friend. Maybe he could become a professional speaker talking about the mistakes he made. He did not have many friends outside of the basketball team, so it dawned on him the brawl with Braden may have been a terrible mistake.

John looked forward getting out of the house on Sunday so he could have a break from thinking too much. He planned to hang out at Don's house that afternoon to watch playoff football. The visit may get his mind off the predicament, even if only for a few moments. He could tell his parents weren't sure how to handle this situation, and they hadn't said much to him all weekend. He had caused so few problems for them over the past few years; John figured they didn't know what to do now that he created havoc just a couple months before leaving home for college. Thankfully, they didn't start handing out punishments or use phrases like, "You're grounded!" or "Don't come out of your room!"

John figured this the visit with the Harmons couldn't have come at a better time. He needed someone to talk to, and he wasn't comfortable talking with his parents. As John cleaned his room, he saw his basketball uniform and realized he should turn it in. A twinge of pain shot through John's chest, realizing the result of his actions. John's parents sent him to the grocery store before his visit to the Harmons. As John worked his way down the aisles, he bumped into Courtney and Amber.

"Hey, aren't you working fast food today," John asked Courtney with a smile.

"Don't remind me," Courtney replied. "I start work in a couple hours. Hey, so I heard something about you getting kicked off the basketball team. What's going on?"

John looked cautiously at both girls, not wanting to ruin his reputation with them. "Yeah, you heard right."

Courtney gave John a confused look. "Why? What did you do?"

"I got into a fight with Braden and then told off the coach. That'll get just about anyone kicked off the team."

"Why would you fight with Braden?" Amber asked. "I thought he was your friend?"

"Not anymore. He's kind of been a jerk this year since he became one of the better players on the team. I finally had enough."

"That's too bad," Amber said.

"Do you mind if I sit by you two at lunch on Monday? I obviously won't be sitting with Braden anymore."

Both girls hesitated before Amber finally said something. "Sure."

John tried to mix in some humor. "Hopefully you two don't mind sitting near a troublemaker. The principals will probably be monitoring my behavior the whole time."

The girls giggled before Courtney smiled while responding. "I guess we'll be OK."

On the ride home, John thought about the impossibility of having some sort of a friendship with these girls when everyone around him probably had nothing good to say about him. He wondered if he could salvage his name with only a few months of school remaining. John quickly put away the groceries he bought as his parents wandered in together.

"John, I'm not sure you should go over to the Harmon's place this afternoon, considering what's going on with you," Betty said in a concerned tone.

Rick jumped in the conversation quickly. "Yeah John, shouldn't you be figuring out how you're going to deal with your situation instead of running off to watch more football? You've watched plenty of football this weekend, anyway. You should be apologizing to the coach and hoping he forgives you."

"I've been sitting at home all weekend. I would really

appreciate it if you'd just let me go over there. I just need someone to talk to. I don't even care about the football game."

"John, why don't you just talk to us?" Betty replied. Maybe we can help you."

"I don't think so. Just let me talk to someone else."

Rick waited a moment to respond. "OK, John, but I'm expecting you to correct whatever problems you've caused. I don't want to hear about more fights or anything else. We thought you had a good head on your shoulders, but you're really making us wonder what kind of person you are."

John bit his tongue, trying not to become angry, because he knew they could ask him to stay home if he said anything objectionable. He just nodded his head and headed toward the door. John jumped into his Ford and drove to a residential neighborhood a few miles from his home. The homes in this neighborhood weren't as new as the ones in Braden's neighborhood, but they were nice. John walked up to the door at the one-floor ranch with wood siding and rang the doorbell. He suddenly became nervous, knowing this could be a long afternoon explaining his problems.

Julie answered the door with a smile. "Hi John, come on in. We have the game on."

Both Don and Julie wore jeans and sweatshirts as they enjoyed their Sunday afternoon. Don sat on a comfortable-looking couch in the living room, where a large flat screen television hung from the wall. Don greeted John as he walked across the white living room carpet, as the crowd noise projecting from the television set provided background noise and their children ran around the house with loud toys.

Don reached for some crackers and cheese on the small table in front of him. "Hey John, come on in and have a seat. The score's already 10-0."

"Hey, thanks for inviting me over, I appreciate it. It's been kind of a rough few days for me. Actually, it's been a rough senior year."

Don turned down the television volume, as if he sensed a conversation coming on. "So, what's up?"

"Well, it's a long story. Are you sure you want to talk now or maybe wait until, like, the football offseason?"

"Of course we can talk now, John. How long have we been friends, right? We want to know what's up."

"All right. This is probably going to be a bit of an awkward story to tell. I messed up this week."

"That's OK. I'm all ears."

"Well, maybe you've noticed, but I've had a difficult time getting used to sitting on the bench all season now that I'm a senior. I also didn't get into State University and have no idea what I want to do with my life. I've just felt pressure this year, and nothing has gone the way I hoped it would. Braden, meanwhile, is doing well with basketball but hasn't exactly been the best friend in the world. He's dating someone who doesn't seem to be very nice, and he wants me to hang out with her friends who I have nothing in common with. And he's always making comments letting me know he's better than me."

Don nodded every few moments, as John continued. "So, the other day in practice I got stuck playing with the backups and, as usual, we turned it over a bunch of times. I tried chasing down Braden after he made a steal, and out of frustration I leveled him as he was going up for a layup. It was the last play of the practice. Braden and I got into a scuffle, and coach kicked me off the team. As I left, I told the coach off. I burned all my bridges in one sitting."

Don laughed, as Julie quietly walked into the living room and sat down on a seat in the corner of the room. John realized she probably wanted to listen but didn't want to intrude.

John gave Don a chance to let it all sink in. "I guess I'm sorry about the way things happened. It's embarrassing getting kicked off the team. Now everyone hates me for being a selfish jerk. I don't know, though, I just couldn't bottle up any more frustration, and it all kind of came out at once. Things started getting out of control, and I just kept going on the attack."

Don looked at John with his usual understanding look. "Yeah, sounds like you're in quite the predicament. So what kind of season were you expecting this year?"

"I just wanted to play some sort of a role. Even if it was for just a couple minutes per game. I didn't care, I just wanted to help the team somehow. Sitting on the bench isn't a role; it's like being a fan. The fans get to watch me sit there with a bunch of juniors who will probably get their turn next season. There is no next season for me, and I just wanted to be part of the team. We're winning games, and all I've done is watch."

Don continued asking questions. "Do you think you should be playing?"

"Yeah, I've been playing for as long as Braden, and I can play. I've always been able to handle the ball, shoot, and I don't commit many turnovers. I played enough minutes on the junior varsity basketball team, so I don't get why I've been overlooked on varsity. I sat on the bench last year but figured I'd finally play some this year."

"So what motivated you to stick with it this year after sitting on the bench last year?"

John looked at Don with a serious expression. "I love basketball. I like everything about it, and I want badly to do well. If I could have any success at all, it would mean a lot to me. It's all I have. I don't really have any other interests."

"So, what's going to happen now that you're not on the team?"

"I don't know, I'll probably drive myself crazy thinking about it. Maybe once I'm in college I can move on from this. It's tough now, though. I don't feel like I have any friends and feel like a complete loser. I guess I've really messed things up."

"Well, there are always going to be consequences for our actions, but we can get back on our feet."

"I don't know. I guess I was looking forward to seeing you guys, because I thought I could get some advice. I don't know what to do, and I just don't feel comfortable talking about it with my parents. They mean well I guess but don't understand me."

"Is basketball the most important thing to you in life?"

John smiled, thinking Don should have been a counselor. "No, I guess not. Maybe at times it feels like it is."

"You know, a lot of us adults have experienced many similar things, but obviously you don't always see us go through them. We now have experience, of course, and can maybe guide others a bit through those same things. We have the gift of hindsight. It's not that we were smarter years ago, and that's why we're doing OK now."

John smiled. "Yeah, it's just tough to see a place in the future where I'll be happy with the way my life is going."

"You know, I played several sports in high school, including basketball. I was a starter on the team, and we did pretty well. Julie played volleyball in high school and was good at it. I had a lot of good times, but I didn't play in college and knew I wasn't going to become a professional, so I just enjoyed it when I did and never thought much more about it. In the long run, everything else was just more important. John, I think you're going to be OK. Maybe you've just lost focus on some of the most important things, though."

"What do you mean?"

"Well, I think someday your priorities might be much different than they are right now."

"I know, but I want to be able to look back and be happy about what I accomplished. I haven't done a darn thing."

"You've accomplished plenty outside of basketball, and you'll have skills to get through life. And remember, some of your teammates may have basketball skills but could lack some of the things you have that will be important in the future."

John nodded.

"Look, the future will be fine as long as you treat people well and live life the way you know you're supposed to live it."

"Yeah, I know. You're right. I guess maybe I lost sight of that a bit, but I just don't feel like things are going to work out. I don't feel like I'm asking for much to play a little basketball and get into college. I don't even care about what college I get into as much as I care about playing basketball. I've invested a lot of time and energy in the sport, and it just feels like it has gone to waste."

"You know, I don't think it has. You'd be surprised by the number of opportunities out there for people who love basketball. Like most people, it will likely mean not playing basketball for a living. You'll always have the opportunity to play basketball in some capacity. You can coach, play in a rec league, cover basketball as a journalist, work for a professional team or get involved in other ways."

John leaned back on the couch, thinking. Don gave John a few seconds before continuing. "Things aren't as hopeless as they seem right now, John. You do have a lot of work ahead to get your focus right and mend some broken relationships, but I think you can do that."

John stared at the ground. "I feel like getting a passport and leaving the country as soon as possible."

Don laughed. "That might only be a temporary solution. People sit on the bench in other countries too. What you might not realize is that you have plenty of good things going. You have good grades, you can get into a lot of colleges. Most kids don't know what they want to do. You don't have to have that figured out. You'll find what career you're looking for later."

"So what do I do, Don? Where do I even start? Like I said, I ruined everything."

"Obviously, you might need some help changing some things in your life so your anger and frustration don't get the best of you in the future. You can't let this happen too often or you might face the same problems again."

"How do I repair any of the damage I've done with everyone at school?"

Don smiled. "I guess I don't have all the answers, but I would recommend honesty. If anyone asks, be honest and apologetic, and maybe in time things will work out."

"I suppose there's no way to fix things with my coach and teammates, right?"

"How long have you known your coach?"

"Years. He coached us during summer basketball since I was in middle school."

"Do you think he'd be receptive to hearing an apology?"

"The dude was pretty mad. He blew a gasket when I got into the fight with Braden. He seemed pretty serious about making sure I didn't come back."

"Why don't you just talk to him? If you apologize and acknowledge the reasons why you were wrong, who knows?"

A mischievous smile crossed John's face. "Sometimes you do know. I told him off pretty good in front of the entire team. What if he takes the opportunity to tell me off?"

"Well, that's a risk you may have to take. How badly do

you want to make things right? Even if you don't get back on the team, at least you'll be able to apologize and let him think about things. Maybe he'll at least understand you better."

"Yeah, you're probably right. That won't be awkward at all, will it?"

Don smiled. "You'll be OK. Your parents will be there for you, and Julie and I are always happy to talk to you."

"So what do you think about all this other stuff? I'm running out of time to find a college."

"You'll figure it out. Many schools would be happy to have you on campus. Your grades are good, I don't think you have anything to worry about."

"Thanks."

"John, you're a good guy. I've seen the way you help others, and you really seem to care about doing the right thing. You're going to be OK. If you can change some things, you're going to be in good shape. This isn't going to be easy facing up to your mistakes, but if you work hard at it, who knows what can happen?"

Julie, who sat quietly, finally chipped in. "John, if there's anything we can do, just let us know, OK?"

"Yeah, I will."

John looked over at the television with the score reading 31-0. "I guess we didn't miss much, huh?"

Don smiled, looking at the television screen.

John became serious once again. "Hey, thanks so much you two, I really appreciate it. I'll give everything a try. Thanks for giving me some ideas. I'll try not to let everyone down again."

Monday morning, John walked up to Coach Thompson's office door at school and took a deep breath before knocking.

Chapter 4

John heard footsteps moving toward the door as his heart rate increased. Coach Thompson opened the door and looked at John while he wrinkled his eyebrows. John gave him a chance to say something but realized he should speak.

"Can we talk?"

Coach Thompson waved his hand, motioning John toward his desk. As they sat down, coach gave John a quizzical look, as if attempting to guess John's motives.

"You're off the team, remember? If you're trying to make a weak attempt to get back on the squad, you can forget it. There's no room for players like you on this team. We're here to win, and you undermined that."

John looked at the floor. "Yeah."

John hesitated before responding. He lifted his head and looked his coach in the eye. "Look, I don't care about that. I just wanted to make things right and apologize. I was selfish and let my frustration get the best of me. It was my fault, and I'm sorry. I was disrespectful toward you and my teammates."

Coach Thompson shook his head. "Will that be all?"

"I just want you to know how much I love basketball, and being off the team made me sick at first, but I realized I messed up and made some changes. I was just frustrated, because it's my senior year and I feel like my window for doing something good for the team is running out, and I lost it. Again, I'm sorry. I should have manned up and knocked on your door before all this happened. I guess I just didn't feel comfortable doing that. Now, it's too late and I burned too many bridges."

John looked at his coach quizzically. "Would you have listened to me if I had stopped by a few weeks ago?"

"Of course."

"I don't know. I just have always had this impression I was just a number and not that important. I guess it doesn't matter."

Coach Thompson became frustrated. "Why would you think that?"

"Well, you just never gave me any advice on how to improve. I just felt like the starting five were the only important players, and I was just there for someone to scrimmage against. I really did want to get better and would have listened. I guess I haven't enjoyed my time on the team much."

"My job is to get the team ready for the game, most importantly those who are going to be playing."

John nodded his head, staring into space.

Coach Thompson continued. "The starters earned the right to play. I'm as impartial as I can be."

"Yeah. How are us backups supposed to get better if we don't run the offense in practice and things like that?"

"Well, you can work out on your own. You should know what the offense is and be ready if needed."

John wanted to argue with him but held his tongue. "OK. Thanks for your time, I appreciate the explanation. I guess I was thinking at the beginning of the year I would be good enough to get a bit of playing time, but so much for that."

"You think you're the first kid who thought he deserved playing time and didn't get it? I've been coaching for quite a few years, and this happens every year. Each player thinks they should be a starter."

"Just out of curiosity, since I'm here, what did I need to improve?"

"Your defense, ball handling, jump shot."

John nodded. "Thanks."

John rose from his seat and headed for the door.

Coach sat back in his chair, watching John open the door. "You know, Braden could have really helped you with your game. Too bad you wanted to fight him instead."

"Yeah, that was my bad, but becoming a star went to his head. All I ever wanted was a couple minutes of playing time each game and that would have been enough for me, but Braden and some of the others don't realize how fortunate they are to get to help the team. Braden was a jerk this year. He became arrogant and belittled me because I wasn't a star like him. That bothered me. I want you to know that. I should have been content just to be on the team and I messed that up. I'm sorry. I'll learn from this, though, and wanted to get this off my chest."

Coach nodded while facing his desk as John shut the door behind him.

Braden walked by John with a couple teammates as students now filled the halls a couple minutes before class. Braden noticed John leaving the coach's office.

"What the heck, man? Isn't that the last place you should be?"

"I needed to apologize."

"I'm not taking any more cheap shots from you, so he better not have let you on the team."

"Look, I know I messed up. Are you guys really going to give me a bad time the rest of my life over that? What I did was stupid, we all know that, but I'm sorry and it will never happen again."

Braden shook his head. "Whatever, you just want to get

back on the team. I would recommend leaving us alone or we'll be the ones doing the cheap shots."

John glared at Braden. "You've been taking cheap shots all year, just with your mouth instead of your muscle. You were constantly giving me a bad time, because you thought I wasn't as good as you."

Braden and the two starters with him, Teyshaun White and DaVonte Keys glared back at him as John continued. "I know I'm the last person who should be asking this, but what happened to you guys? I make a mistake and you treat me like garbage when I try to apologize? No one's perfect, and I'm not going to be jealous of anyone anymore just because they can play ball. I was, but I'm over it. I hope you're all going to the NBA, because otherwise you'll realize you can't treat everyone like garbage who isn't a superstar. I'm sorry about what I did, but if you can't accept an apology I'm not going to be desperate for your approval. Have a good one."

As John headed to class, he noticed Coach Thompson peeking through his door at the conversation between the former teammates. John wondered how much of the conversation he heard. Throughout classes that day, John had trouble concentrating and instead thought about all that transpired. He wondered if he could actually be content not being on the team the rest of the season or whether this would eat at him the rest of the year.

John nervously walked through the lunch room a couple hours later, looking for Amber and Courtney. He wondered how this would go and if they wanted to be friends with him. John walked up to their table, holding his lunch.

"Hello, could you two tell me if this is the spot you're interviewing for a new friend?"

Courtney looked at John. "This is, but I looked at your application, and I don't think you're interview-worthy."

"Ouch. But my application says that my only weakness is that sometimes I care too much."

John sat down and began eating, listening to the two girls talk. "Hey, so I talked to the basketball coach today. I think he might be considering letting me back on the team."

"That's awesome!" Amber responded. "He seems like he's a tough coach."

"Yeah, he's no-nonsense. Although I've never met a coach was a 'nonsense' coach."

"What would one of those be like?" Courtney asked with a smile.

"You know, putting whoopee cushions on the bench before games. Maybe tripping someone during sprints and then laughing at them, and of course practicing trick shots during pre-game warm-ups. I think a lot of players would enjoy a coach who's all nonsense."

"You probably wouldn't have gotten kicked off the team," Courtney said under her breath.

"Thanks," John said sarcastically. "I appreciate that."

The final school bell finally rang as John headed to his locker to grab his books and leave. John walked by Coach Thompson as he unlocked one of the gym doors as he wheeled a cart of basketballs into the gym. He looked at John passing by and waved him over.

"Hey, so I have a couple things I need to think about. I'll get back to you in a couple days, OK."

"Uh, yeah, OK. Sounds good."

John walked away perplexed, not sure what to make of his coach's comments. Was he going to let him back on the team? Hopefully he wasn't going to make him the towel guy out of pity or something. He could only imagine the beating he'd take from the guys having to bring them water.

John arrived home and finished homework, getting his

work done so he could head for the YMCA that night to shoot hoops. He figured he'd better stay in basketball shape in the rare chance he ended up back on the team. As John finished dinner, his mother answered a ringing phone.

"John, it's for you."

John finished his bite of food and answered.

"Hey John," Don Harmon's friendly voice greeted him.

"Hi, how's it going?"

"You talk to Coach Thompson?"

"Yeah, we had a good talk. It's tough to know what he's thinking, but I survived it. I apologized but also let him know what I had been frustrated with. He didn't scream at me, so I guess that's a good sign."

"Well good, keep up the fight to get back on the right track. Julie and I are proud of you, John. You're doing the right thing, and even though you may not realize it, you're setting yourself up well for the future. I'll talk to you later, OK?"

"Yeah, thanks Don."

The basketball swished through the net later that night as sweat dripped from John's shirt. He wiped some of the wetness off his forehead with the side of his shirt and looked into the adjacent workout room at the YMCA. He didn't see anyone he knew this evening. No Amber, no classmates. Just him and the basketball hoop with students from other schools playing at the other baskets.

"This is a chance to improve my game," John thought. "It's now or never. Either I make some improvements or it could be too late."

John worked on jumpers and ball handling while remembering his coach's words about what he could improve. After an hour of jump shooting, John looked over at a group of students looking at him from a nearby hoop. One guy in the group walked toward him as he dribbled the basketball. The student approached John slowly while his friends watched.

"Hey, what school you from?"

John picked up his basketball. "North."

"Why are you here?"

"Just working on my game. It needs plenty of work."

"Huh. You on the team?"

"Not at the moment."

"Why?"

"Long story. What school you guys from?"

"East High."

"Oh yeah, you guys have a good team."

"Yeah, we're the best."

"You on the team?"

"No, a couple of us tried out for the team but didn't make it. I'm sure we'd have made the cut if we played for your team, though."

"You sure about that?"

"Hey, at least we'll be rooting on the state champion. We're the deepest team in the state, so don't plan on a victory party."

"Well, it's not like I'll have much to do with it, but neither will you it looks like. Your team is good, but you're not even the best in the conference, so I wouldn't count on state."

"Don't make me and my boys come over and kick your butt man."

"Yeah, all right. Have a good night."

John turned toward the hoop and floated a shot toward the rim.

"Everybody's thinks they're the greatest," John muttered to himself. "And when I admit I'm not the greatest, everyone's quick to agree."

After running sprints to exhaustion, John drove home wondering if any of this effort would be worth it. John drove through his city, street lights aglow with little traffic this time of night. John thought about how nice it would be to have a few more friends. He told himself to hang in there and that college might do wonders to advance his floundering social life.

Tuesday morning, John found his seat in class early going over some notes. Braden arrived early, as well, surprising John.

John smiled to himself. "Since when did Braden arrive anywhere early? Maybe he's flunking or something."

Braden sat down a few seats away from John, pretending not to see him. John took a deep breath.

"You know, this is stupid, Braden. Someday you're going to realize people make mistakes and that you have to get over it."

"Whatever, no one likes you, John."

"Well, besides the fact that's not true, at least I now know who cares about me and who is only nice to someone if they're, say, on the basketball team. How many people would be hanging out with you if you weren't starting? I'd tell you to take some time to think about that, but I'm sure it won't concern you too much."

"No, it doesn't. I don't plan on attacking someone in practice anytime soon."

"Yeah, well you've been a piece of work since you became a starter. Your ego is becoming like the blob or something. It's taking over the whole town."

"Whatever."

John decided reasoning with Braden did not work at this point and did not bug him anymore. He instead thought about what coach might talk to him about. He hoped Coach Thompson's call arrived sooner rather than later so he could put his worry to rest. He knew he shouldn't worry and that it would not do him one minute of good to do so, but he could not help it at times.

"Whatever happens, happens," John muttered to himself as he walked into the lunch room. He found a spot by Amber and Courtney, and smiled to himself thinking about how this is his favorite part of the day. A few days earlier, John invited the freshman Steve to sit with them. At first, Steve sat timidly, listening to the group of girls talk but returned each lunch despite his obvious discomfort. John noticed him become more comfortable each lunch, even though he still didn't say much. Several other girls, friends of Courtney and Amber, sometimes joined Courtney and Amber and did plenty of talking. The group of girls talked about topics uninteresting to John, but he felt comfortable knowing he did not have to lead the round table discussion. As several of the girls chatted, John leaned over to Amber.

"Forgot to tell you, Coach Thompson's going to call me in next couple days. Not sure what he wants to discuss, but it can't be a bad thing. Maybe he wants me to be the ball boy or something."

"Oh, OK. Do you think he got over everything?"

"Who knows?"

A faint smiled traced Amber's lips. "So, will you be OK if you don't get to play basketball again?"

"Yeah, I'll only need minor psychiatric help. I can't pay too much, though. What's your going rate? You probably give good advice."

"Don't know if I can help you there."

A serious look crossed John's face, thinking more about the question. "I could always play just for fun in intramural basketball or something in college. I'll survive, grow up, get a job and forget all about it like all the other adults who are former jocks."

"You don't sound too happy."

"I just miss playing. That's why I'm down at the YMCA every darn day working out. I really need more hobbies or something."

"So you really have no idea what you want to do after college?"

"No, but not that many students do, so I'll figure it out."

"What if you get a couple years in and still don't know?"

"I thought that's why colleges have philosophy majors? No, I'll figure something out."

That evening, John returned home from working out after school at the YMCA and nearly finished his homework when the phone rang.

John's mother yelled from the kitchen phone. "John! It's for you."

John made his way across the living room and grabbed the phone.

"This is John."

"Hey John, this is Coach Thompson."

A sweat broke across John's forehead, knowing his next few months might be determined by this conversation.

Chapter 5

John took a deep breath and asked the key question. "So, what's up?"

"Yeah, I said I would call you after deciding what I should do with your case. I have to say, I've coached for a number of years and haven't encountered this. Most of the students who cause trouble don't show much remorse. Most of the guys who lose their spot on the team do off the court stuff, rather than something in practice.

"Glad to hear I'm an original."

"So here's the deal. I'll give you a chance to prove you can handle being on the team. Obviously it goes without saying if you mess up, it will be game over for you."

"Yeah, of course."

"Any thoughts on how to make amends with your teammates?"

"Should I get them each a new car? Wait, I can't afford that. Maybe a Hot Wheels® one."

"Whatever you do, you'll need to figure something out, because it could be a long rest of the season if your teammates hate you."

"Yeah, they're pretty mad at me right now. The last thing they want is me back on the team."

"You got yourself into this and now you have to get yourself out of it."

"Thanks coach, I won't let the team down."

John broke the news to his parents that night at dinner,

hoping they'd be pleased.

"So coach is giving me another chance," John said in the middle of a bite of bread.

His parents looked at him quizzically for a moment before his father got in the first word.

"Well, you better make him and the team not regret this. I still don't know why you even want to bother at this point. Why not just focus on your studies and get ready for college that's coming up fast?"

"I've tried telling you, I like basketball. This may be my last chance to play for a team before having to just play for fun."

"Maybe fun is what you need," John's mother added to the conversation. "This organized stuff doesn't seem to make you happy."

John shrugged off the comment and finished his dinner before heading off to the YMCA for another workout. Once there, John worked hard to get ready for his return to the team, shooting, dribbling and trying to perfect everything the coach said he needed to improve. At the nearby baskets, a group of high schoolers from another school loudly organized a pickup game. One of the boys yelled across to John.

"Hey, we need one more to make 10, you in?"

John thought for a moment, considering whether he should. "Sure."

"Alright, you better bring your 'A' game against us," the same student responded with a smile. "I don't think you can handle a team with this much game."

John smiled, wondering to himself how this game will go against a bunch of guys he doesn't know.

A few minutes into the game, he realized this might be a good warm-up to getting back into shape for basketball practice. One of the guys, in an effort to show off, tried to dribble through his legs as John guarded him. He tipped the ball away from the player and dribbled down court for an easy layup.

"Hey, what are you doing? I was about to put a move on you?" The young man said from over a half court away.

"What do you expect me to do when you put the ball out there like that?" John replied with a wide grin on his face. "This isn't street ball! I'm not going to stand there and let you dribble around for half an hour."

John started hitting shots on the less-than-stellar defense that often accompanies pickup games. The opposing team's best player started getting after his teammates.

"Hey, you gotta step out on him. You can't just let him shoot like that."

"I couldn't get around the pick, I needed you to step out on him," the player responded defensively, pointing at another teammate."

"Me? You could have stepped through that, but you just stopped."

John smiled at the banter as he dribbled down court. Feeling good about his game, he hoisted a three from several feet behind the arc. The shot felt off, but it hit the backboard and went in.

"Come on, that ain't fair," his opponent offered, afraid of a response from his teammate, who did not hesitate to criticize him once again.

"OK, I guess I'll guard him since you can't play defense," the exasperated leader of the team stated. He waved his hand showing his teammate who to guard. "OK, you take him instead. I'll guard this new guy."

He stood in front of John with a business-like expression on his face. "Alright, happy-go-fun time is over. I'm here to shut you down."

John smiled, ready to respond. "You couldn't shut down an

ice cream truck, man."

"You're done."

A few plays later, John got the ball off a screen as his opponent fought through the pick to stay with him. John faked a shot, sending him jumping high in the air as John took a couple dribbles to the basket and sunk a jump shot. It took just a second before his opponents got after their vocal teammate.

"Dude, I thought you had him? What happened man?"

"Shut up!" was all he could muster, looking a bit embarrassed.

"At least you got a good look at the ceiling," John added with a big grin on his face. "I should have given you a dust rag to do some cleaning since it looks like it's been awhile since the rafters have been touched."

For the first time in a long while, John felt happy to play basketball. His slightly inferior opponents may have had something to do with this temporary pleasure, but John was happy to settle for a moment of joy. As John headed out for the evening, he heard a familiar voice coming from a workout bike.

"Hey, I saw you playing basketball," Amber said while continuing her workout as her pal Courtney role the bike next to her. "It looked like you were having fun. Basketball isn't so hard, is it?"

"Basketball is supposed to be fun, right?" John replied. "When are you going to show me how it's done, All-Star?"

"I don't want to show off," Courtney said with a smile.

"Ah, you're so humble. I don't know if you know this about me or not, but humility is my favorite quality about myself."

Courtney snickered, as Amber tried to maintain a serious face. "No, I didn't know that. You probably hate people who brag about themselves, right?"

"Yeah, I hate hearing people talk about themselves. I just always think, 'Enough about yourself. Let's talk about me.' Oh, speaking of which, I'm back on the team, so when you coming out to a game?"

"Wait, you're back on the team? When did this happen?" Amber responded.

"Earlier today. I apologized for the manner in which I conducted myself and offered to mow coach's lawn the rest of his life. OK, not the last part, but I did tell him I can change my ways."

Courtney laughed. "Do boys ever really change? I thought they stay immature forever."

John wore a mock offended look on his face. "So cynical at such a young age. I can change. Yesterday I wore a different pair of pants, so see? I don't play with action figures anymore or eat animal crackers. I kind of regret giving up the crackers, though, they're still good."

Both girls shook their heads, wearing smiles.

"Honestly, I haven't been to a game all year," Amber said, as Courtney admitted the same.

"Really? Then why do you both have my poster on your walls? You know, the one where I'm wearing a cape and sitting in a convertible? Seriously, you should stop by. If seven players foul out, I'm the third guy off the bench."

The girls looked at each other.

"I'm not much of a basketball fan," Courtney said.

"Well, you can learn a bit more. Plus, there's people and popcorn! I gotta go, but good seeing you and I'll catch you tomorrow."

"Good night," both girls echoed.

As John closed his locker on the way to class the next morning, he spotted the freshman he had tried to befriend, to little avail. Steve carried the solemn expression he seemed to always wear, as if he were merely trying to survive each passing minute. John didn't hold it against him, considering his freshman status and the tough times he faced. Watching Steve helped him realize that his own suffering is just relative to others' problems. Compared to him, John's life seemed fantastic.

"Hey Steve, what's new?"

Steve got right to the point. "My grandfather died."

"I'm sorry. When's the funeral?"

"In a few days I guess."

"I know things are tough right now, but hang in there. Things will get better."

"I don't know."

John didn't know what else to say. He didn't know what to say to someone who just lost their grandfather. Should he say "Hey, I'm sure tomorrow will be great!"

"Well, if you need anyone to talk to, let me know. I'm guessing you were close to your grandfather?"

"Yeah, I saw him all the time."

"I'm sorry," John added as the two headed to their respective classes.

John hoped Steve could figure some things out in the next couple years so he wouldn't have to talk him off a ledge or something. While sitting at lunch with Amber and Courtney, John spotted Steve sitting silently with a few other guys. He guessed he was more comfortable sitting with them than with upperclassmen like his group. They all sat silently eating, looking around nervously as if something bad could happen at any minute. Maybe he would feel the same way at basketball practice a little later.

"Poor guy," Courtney said as John explained the situation to the girls.

"Yeah, I hope his life is not like a horror movie sequel

where the killer keeps going after the same person movie after movie. You hope something goes right eventually."

"That's the best analogy you've got?" Courtney said, laughing. "There's no killer chasing him!"

"What about the bully?" John said defensively. "He could be the hypothetical killer I'm talking about."

"I'm not sure I want to talk about killers," Amber interjected. "It's kind of scary."

"The dude just has bad luck," John said. "Like in those same horror movies where the car doesn't start and you're stuck in the middle of the woods."

Later that afternoon, John jogged out to the court that afternoon hoping to get through this most awkward of scenarios. His teammates wasted little time getting the party started. Joe Anthony and Rashad Alexander looked at John and laughed. They looked over at Braden, who worked on his layups at another basket.

"Hey Braden!" Rashad exclaimed. "John wants to know if he can make those layups a bit more challenging. You keep shooting and he'll push you from behind, how does that sound?"

Joe complimented his fellow starter's comments with laughter, looking at John.

John looked at Rashad. "How about I kick your butt? How would you like that?"

"You're going to fight me? I don't think that would be a good thing to do right now."

John just shook his head, somewhat embarrassed. He looked at Joe and Rashad with a slight smile. "Do you think he'd be nervous if I wore brass knuckles?"

"Knowing you, he probably would, right?" Joe asked.

"No, come on man, I'm a changed guy. You're going to let one fit of rage define me?"

The two guys looked at each other.

"Well, yeah, that was pretty bad," Joe explained. "You were, like George Brett running out of the dugout or Roberto Alomar spitting on the ump. Tough to forget that. So yeah, you're that guy."

"Darn," John said, slumping his shoulders comically. "Do you think I can at least get some sponsors due to my image? I could help promote professional wrestling or an action movie marathon on TV. Got to find some way to profit off my bad decisions. Isn't that the American way?"

"Could you please do sponsorships instead of being on the basketball team?" Rashad requested. "We don't need an angry third-stringer."

John looked at Rashad. "You look a lot angrier than me right now. I'm actually quite content."

A few minutes later Coach Thompson beckoned the team to gather at mid-court.

"OK, so I wanted to let everyone know John is back on the team if he behaves himself. I really wasn't going to have him back after the little incident, but John seems to care about the team and deeply regrets the incident that took place. I'm willing to give a second chance and hope you guys are good with this. No one's perfect, so this is a chance for all of us to show some humility. John, do you have anything to add?"

"Yeah, I do. I messed up, guys. I was pretty mad at about a lot of stuff that day and am sorry. I can promise you it won't happen again. Can I buy you all ice cream or something?"

"Yeah, you're sorry you got kicked off the team, huh?" Joe muttered loudly enough for the coach to hear.

"Hey, knock it off!" Coach Thompson shouted. "You guys are going to have to figure it out, because we can't have a bunch of fighting if we're going to have a great season, OK? I know John has a responsibility to regain your trust, but you guys have to give him another chance."

John joined a group of guys playing defense against the starters as they ran through their offense. Joe set a tough pick on John, throwing his elbow at him. John shook it off, but Rashad threw his own illegal pick, knocking him to the ground.

"Plenty more of that coming your way."

John didn't look at him and walked the other way after picking himself up off the ground.

"Why did I think this would be a good idea?" John thought. "I'd be better off trying to be a snake charmer."

After enduring the practice where several teammates took shots at him, John figured he better at least win over his bench mates. If he can't do that, then this will be an embarrassing and lonely way to end the season. As practice ended, John jogged by Coach Thompson, he said "Thanks coach."

After what John endured, he might as well have thanked his teammates, too, after each push and shove. Coach Thompson was simply the organizer of the beating it seemed.

"So how did practice go?" John's dad asked coldly while whipping his mouth with a napkin.

"It was rough, but I knew it was coming."

"You ready to give up this nonsense and focus on where you're going to school next year?"

"Nope. It's not interfering with my studies, and I'll figure out where to go to school soon enough. And I wish you would stop asking me to quit."

John wondered if his father could comprehend anyone having a hobby outside of reading a newspaper each night or spending extra time working. He secretly hoped he would be a bit different than his dad when he got to that age instead of living a predictable existence. Maybe he would be fall into a dull routine at some point and not even realize it. He figured he'd better do something with his life now before he falls into the trap of adulthood.

Thursday morning, John found Steve near his locker before classes began.

"Hey Steve, what are you doing Saturday night?"

"Nothin'. I have a funeral later today."

"Why don't you bring a couple of the guys you sit with at lunch and go to a movie with me and some friends this weekend? I'm inviting Amber and Courtney, as well. It'll give you a chance to get your mind off everything."

"I don't know."

"Come on, if you say 'no' to this, I may give up trying to invite you," John said grinning.

"I'll see, maybe I can."

"Let me know soon so I can plan it out. See you later."

John then strolled over to Courtney and Amber.

"Hey girls, I just invited Steve and a couple of his friends to join us Saturday night."

"Saturday night?" Courtney asked.

"Yeah, can you join me for a movie?"

The two girls looked at each other.

"Come on, I can't spend Saturday night with only freshmen."

"Yeah, we don't have anything planned, I guess we could go," Courtney concluded.

"Thank goodness," John smiled with an exaggerated sigh of relief. "This organizing stuff is difficult. Two different groups of people, it's brutal."

"What are we going to see?" Amber asked.

"That new one that has it all – adventure, action, bad people who must be punished."

"I think I saw the ad for that, it looks OK." Courtney questioned.

"It will be better with Amber making sarcastic comments throughout," John added.

"What makes you think I'd do that?" Amber said innocently.

"Because you only like revenge movies."

"What?"

"I know about you. You have voodoo dolls that look like everyone in the high school, and you also watch those television series about women who kill just for the fun of it."

"How do you know about that?" Amber asked smiling.

"That's what my sources tell me, and believe me, I have lots of them. My teammates are willing to say negative things about anyone if I ask."

"So what time?" Amber inquired.

"I think there's a six o'clock showing."

"Why did you pick a movie?" Courtney wondered.

"Give me a break, what else is there to do in this town when the weather's cold? It's not like we can host a garden party. If you have a better idea, please let me know."

"A garden party?" Courtney asked. "Are we old people?"

"OK, so maybe we wouldn't do that no matter what time of year it is."

"Let's plan for a movie then," Amber stated.

Friday evening, John suited up for the first time in what felt like forever. None of his teammates, even those who rode the bench with him, spoke to him.

"Gentlemen of the board," Sam Stevens announced. "Let us now begin this meeting."

"Glad to see not too much has changed," John said to Dominique with a wide grin. Dominique just nodded, focusing on the court.

The Leopards hosted Riverfront, one of the toughest teams in the conference and struggled early. Coach Thompson was in rare form that night, irked from the opening tip by his team's play. John turned to Dominique with a smile.

"Is it just me or is coach's face turning redder by the minute? He does that every time he talks to me, but this is unusual."

Dominique didn't seem to see the humor in his comments, but added "Maybe if we grabbed a rebound once in a while he wouldn't have to yell."

John decided now was as good a time as any to ask some questions.

"Hey, so does everyone on the team hate me or what? I know I lost my temper, but I kind of doubt Braden's nice to you guys."

"I don't know, man," Dominique said distantly.

"You guys gotta give me another chance, I'm going to be on the bench with you the rest of this season. It's gonna suck with no one to talk to. I won't screw up again. You saw all the crap I took the other day from the starters. They were throwing elbows and everything. I can take it all season without losing it, I guarantee it.

"What, are you Joe Namath or something, guaranteeing success?"

"It's not like guaranteeing a Super Bowl win, I'm just determined not to screw up."

"Good luck with that."

"I figure I better not set the bar too high, like wanting to get in the game or something."

If Coach Thompson's mood was an indicator, John could tell it was not North High's night. The Leopard's did not play well, turning the ball over and not giving a solid effort on defense. Inside the halftime locker room, Coach Thompson let the team hear about it.

"You guys aren't rebounding, helping on defense or making

solid passes!" Coach Thompson yelled, as his face turned a deeper shade of red. "What in the world are you doing out there? I didn't come to the gym here tonight to lose at home to a team we can beat. You better snap out of it, or it's going to be a long practice on Monday!"

John hoped this effort had nothing to do with the team's sour disposition over his return. He looked over at several of the starters, including Braden, with their heads down and sapped of energy. The Leopards did not snap out of it after halftime, continuing to make the same mistakes that plagued them in the first half. John turned to Juan Hernandez, who sat to his left, as the team trailed by 10 points with three minutes left.

"Try again next time, huh?"

Juan shook his head, clearly frustrated by the team's loss. He had played just a few minutes, not able to give the team a jolt of energy.

"You don't think it's my return to the team, do you?" John tried to joke.

Juan didn't respond, either not in the mood to talk or still ticked at John.

Coach Thompson said fewer words after the game but ones that silenced the team.

"We're going back to work on Monday, so be prepared for some running and more running."

"Great," thought John. "Just what I signed up for."

"The beatings will continue until morale improves," Sam announced quietly.

John looked over at his teammates, who he figured would have loved to run a bit more during the game tonight as opposed to practice on Monday. At least he had Saturday night to look forward to. After finishing the last of his homework the following evening, John felt a bit more relaxed, knowing he had the rest of the weekend to have some fun. His parents went off to visit some relatives during the day Saturday, so he watched television and readied for his little get-together that evening. Steve gave him the OK for joining him and convinced one of his friends to join him. He figured he would have just enough room in his small Ford Focus for the trip. At least it was better than having to transport friends in his parents' Buick LeSabre.

After picking up Steve, John asked him where his friend, Henry, lived. Luckily, it wasn't far from Steve's place. Both girls owned cars, but allowed John to give them a ride. He felt like a taxi driver, making several stops picking up one person a time. Steve picked Amber up first, letting her sit in the front seat while the two freshmen sat in back. When Courtney hopped in the car, she slid into the back seat behind John.

"Hey, how did Amber get the passenger's seat?"

"Luck of the draw, I guess," John replied, smiling at Amber. She said she's the best navigator in the city."

John looked over at Amber, looking to break the silence that permeated the car. "You're not going to blame me if the movie's horrible, are you?"

"Why, do you think it's going to be bad?"

"I hope not, I need to catch a break for once. I've been blamed for enough stuff this semester. Our team's loss last night won't help any, either. We're going to have a painful practice on Monday."

"Wait, you guys lost last night?" Courtney chimed in from the back seat.

"Sorry to hear that," Amber said.

"I actually don't feel that guilty, considering I only sat and watched. That's like blaming a fan for his team's loss. Maybe the dream of making it to state wasn't so realistic after all."

The movie turned out to be good, as John treated the nontalking guys and female classmates to candy. The evening went faster than John had hoped but invited the group to grab a bit to eat at an ice cream and burger place nearby. The group agreed and they soon found a seat in the back booth of the restaurant, which only had a few groups of students milling about at 8:30 on a Saturday night.

John thought to himself, "Hey, I'm actually having fun."

Sitting next to Amber at the theatre helped, as he made a few comments to her throughout the film, even getting a few laughs from her.

As they relaxed in the booth, John decided to ask about their future plans. "So question for you, Amber and Courtney. Do you think Peter Pan is a superhero or not? Wait, wrong question. Do you know where you're going to school next year?"

"Yeah, actually we want to room together at Southeast Missouri Community College," Courtney explained. "We're going to start there and then transfer to a four-year school."

"Really, how big of a school is that?"

"About a couple thousand, I think," Amber added.

"How hard is it to get in there?" John inquired.

"Why, are you not smart enough to get in anywhere else?" Courtney joked.

"If that's the only place I could get in, what does that say about you?" John shot back with a smile.

"He has a point," Amber said quietly with a smirk.

"So next question," John said. "Would you be OK with me applying there as well? I kind of have no idea what I'm doing and need to figure things out pretty quickly so I can get my parents off my back."

"Should we let him apply?" Courtney said, turning to Amber.

"I suppose it wouldn't make me too mad," Amber replied.

"Are you going to school just to make your parents happy?"

"No, I didn't mean to say it like that. I plan to work hard and graduate. There's just one small problem, I have no idea what I want to major in or do when I get out of college. Maybe that's why I should start at a school like that."

"Yeah, I'm sure you'll be among friends there," Amber said encouragingly. "Many students there aren't sure what they'll major in. You'll have time to figure it out."

"OK, maybe I'll apply as soon as I can. Just out of curiosity, do they have a basketball team?"

"I don't know," Courtney said dismissively. "Why do you care about that, considering all the pain you've suffered in high school basketball?"

"I don't know, I just like to play. Maybe they'll have an intramural team where lousy players who think they are good talk a bunch of trash."

Just as John finished his sentence, an unwanted visitor broke their friendly conversation.

"You now hanging out with the freshmen I like to beat up, Zander?"

John didn't respond to his favorite bully, Matt, who went out of his way to stir up trouble as his two oversized friends snickered from the other side of the restaurant. John just looked up at him, letting Matt make a fool of himself.

"So I get two freshmen to beat up for the price of one? And I get to whoop a senior in front of two girls who should know better than to hang out with three losers."

Matt looked over at the two girls, since no one said anything. "Hey, if you want a good time, come hang out with me and my buddies over there. We'll show you a good time. I hope you like four-wheeling at night. After that, we can make out. John here can watch if he wants."

John got up and started to head to the front of the eatery in search for a manager. The last thing he wanted was a confrontation after all the trouble he seemed to find lately.

Matt pushed John as he tried to walk by.

"Where are you going, Zander?"

Matt then pushed him up against another table as he kept walking toward the front.

"Come on, man, just let it go," John said. "You're not impressing anybody other than your overfed friends over there."

"You calling us fat, Zander?"

"Well, let me know when you make a swimsuit calendar," John replied.

With that, Matt took a swing, hitting John in the nose. Blood immediately ran from his nostrils, but that didn't keep John from giving him a hard push as he bolted toward the food counter. A middle-aged manager had just poked his head out to see what kind of trouble brewed.

"Hey, this guy is harassing my friends and I," John said through labored breaths.

No sooner had John said something than Matt pushed John's head into the counter.

"Hey, knock it off!" the manager yelled at Matt.

The young bullies' friends, who initially watched Matt's efforts, finally spoke.

"Looks like he's had enough," one of the guys, who wore a grungy blue t-shirt and jeans and a smile said. "Let's get out of here, I don't want my dad yelling at me again."

John, with his head pressed against the counter, realized he wasn't getting out of this without some aggression. Matt pushed the manager away with one hand as he was about to intervene. John threw a shot at Matt's chin, causing him to loosen his grip on John's head. He took advantage, throwing a punch at his mid-section with all his force. Matt grunted and staggered backward before lunging at John, who out of the corner of his eye saw the manager reach for a phone. John tried to duck and caught a punch in the shoulder before realizing he'd need to keep fighting. John had enough and decided to take his best shot. He threw a punch that landed on Matt's chin, knocking him backward. John lunged forward throwing another punch, this one to the nose of his stunned opponent, who did not anticipate John's aggressive response. He leaped on Matt, taking him to the ground and began throwing a steady stream of punches before getting up and walking away. Matt tried to get to his feet but instead rolled over and tried to pull himself up.

"This ain't over, John," Matt huffed, wiping blood from his nose with a napkin.

"It never is, is it Matt?" John asked angrily. "Your life must really suck if you have to look for people to beat up. Enjoy the rest of your life in prison, dude. You can fight there every day."

Matt grabbed a burger from a table that cleared out once they saw the fight and threw it at John's friends.

"Real nice," John muttered.

A police officer walked through the door, eliciting a "Thank goodness," from John.

"What's going on here?" the officer questioned.

"This nice young man Matt here decided to interrupt our dinner by attacking me and insulting my friends.

The manager and John's friends backed up his story as Matt continued to hurl insults at John in front of the officer, revealing his lack of control. The officer took Matt out of the restaurant, leaving John and his friends to regroup.

"Well, I think our night of fun just came to an end," John said, stating the obvious. "I'm really sorry about this."

"What in the world, John?" Courtney exclaimed.

"I saw Matt bullying Steve one day and asked him to stop. Needless to say, he added me to his hit list and decided to let us have it tonight. Just my luck to pick the same restaurant this guy goes to. Maybe I need to choose nicer places."

"I'm sure they'll be able to clean up the blood," Amber responded, smiling.

"They could say it's Ketchup," John joked.

Steve wore an angry glare on his face. "I hate that guy."

"Yeah, well, I'm going to have to let the school know about this. Hopefully they can do something about it."

The police officer chatted with the group, getting their side of the story. The restaurant manager told the officer what took place, pitting further evidence against Matt and his friends. John held napkins to his bloodied nose as he watched the officer in action.

John dropped off Henry before pulling into Steve's driveway.

"Hey, I'm sorry about Matt bothering us. He won't be at school much longer, so don't let it get you down. I hope you had a good time tonight despite the brawl."

"Yeah, the movie was cool, see ya."

As the door closed, John looked at the girls.

"Did he say a complete sentence?"

Both girls laughed.

"Yeah, I think so," Courtney replied. "Next time maybe you'll get two. Can you drop me off next, I need to get home. My parents thought I'd be home by about nine and it's, like, 10."

"Sure thing," John said, looking forward to spending a few minutes with Amber.

John's car finally pulled into Courtney's driveway. Her house impressed him, it was a two-story in a nice neighborhood, a lot newer than the homes than the residences that adored John's street. Amber's home was similar to Courtney's house, and nicer than John's residence.

"Thanks again for hanging out, tonight," John said politely as Courtney unhooked her seat belt.

"Yeah, most of it was fun. Let's not invite Matt next time."

"I don't remember giving him an invitation, but I agree."

As John drove slowly down the lit streets towards Amber's home, he apologized once again for the fight.

"Don't worry about it. Not much you could have done, the guy's a jerk. Trouble seems to follow you, huh?"

"Just this semester, apparently," John said quietly, looking down at his bloody knuckles. "I'm really not that horrible of a person. I lost my temper with Braden. I was frustrated about a whole bunch of things, and it just kind of boiled over at one bad practice. He's changed since he became a starter and acts like a big shot. Even if I hadn't gotten mad at him, I think he would have ditched me to hang out with only the starters. He's got a reputation to uphold, I guess. Anyway, it's just been a tough year. I won't get angry again, I'll hang in there."

Amber just nodded her head quietly.

"I really appreciate you and Courtney hanging out with me, though, it's been the best thing this year," John admitted.

"Really?"

"Yeah, I've pretty much just hung out with basketball guys growing up but that changed this semester."

"So why did you start talking to us?"

"You both seemed like nice people. I figured I should try to meet new people."

"Was that the only reason?"

John hesitated to answer the question as he pulled into Amber's driveway.

"OK, I'll admit it didn't hurt that you were good looking," John said with a smile.

Amber blushed, tucking her red hair behind her ear.

John felt beads of nervous sweat start to form on his forehead. He had gone this far, now seemed like a good time to go for broke, despite not feeling like the coolest guy because of the bruised nose and blood on his hands. He took a deep breath and decided to go for it.

"Can I ask you something?"

"Sure."

"Would I be able to take you on a real date sometime soon? I'll try to make sure no violent incidents happen during that time, just for you!"

"Yeah, I'd like that," Amber replied sheepishly but with a smile.

"Great, that'll be fun."

Amber stepped out of the car. "Try not to get in anymore fights on the way home, OK?"

"What, don't you like hanging out with people with facial bruises? People will think I'm tough."

"I prefer nice over tough."

"That's a good call, see you Sunday."

John drove away with a smile and a sense of relief. "Finally something good has happened for the first time in a while," John thought to himself. "Maybe I won't mess this up like I did basketball."

Chapter 6

John slapped an ice pack on his nose and plopped down on the couch, turning on a couple of lights in the dark and silent house. His parents retired for the evening well before his return. John's head swirled with the evening's events. A new girlfriend, a fight and a college possibility all in an evening's work. Usually his life moved at the speed of a turtle.

Sunday afternoon, John found the motivation to apply to his friends' school and research its basketball team. He planned to contact the basketball coach, because he figured they might need a water boy or something. He hoped this would work out, because if not he'd have to start filling out more applications. After spending several hours filling out the paperwork, John felt a sense of accomplishment.

"I can't imagine applying to 10 schools," John said to himself. "I wouldn't have time to do my homework and would flunk out of school by trying to get into college."

Monday morning arrived with John knocking on the principal's door, trying to avert any trouble he may inherit due to Saturday night's incident.

"Come on in," the principal said, not looking up from his papers until John walked in and took a seat."

"Hi John, how may I help you?" the principal stated while peering at John through his glasses.

John felt a bit intimidated sitting across from Mr. Charles, who wore a white dress shirt and tie. John wondered if the principal's receding hairline reflected years of stress at the school.

"I just wanted to let you know about an incident that took place Saturday night. I was out at a restaurant with friends when the infamous Matt Mathews just randomly attacked us. I had to fight back to protect my friends. He's been bullying people for a long time and he decided he didn't like me because I asked him to stop bullying a freshman earlier this year."

"Yes, I heard about the matter" the principal replied.

John reacted nervously, rubbing his hands on his jeans.

"Are you OK?"

"Yeah, I got a bloody nose, though. My friends and the restaurant manager can vouch for what happened. The freshman Matt bullied was with my two other friends. He approached us and started the fight when we were just sitting there eating."

"I believe that's what happened, but what's going on with you, John? You get kicked off the basketball team and now fights?"

"I'm back on the basketball team," John replied defensively. "I don't know what I could have done differently. Should I have just let him shove everyone around? The dude's violent and is just going to continue messing with everyone. The police took him away, so I would think this should be taken seriously."

"Yes, absolutely. I was just asking, because you seem to be in the middle of stuff lately."

"I didn't go looking for this one. Matt was pushing Steve around in the middle of the school and someone needed to step in."

"Thanks for stopping it," Mr. Charles stated. "Try to keep out of fights."

As he left the office, John tried to forget his continued issues with the big bad bully Matt and his sore nose as the basketball team practiced for a road game the following evening. John still couldn't get used to teammates not talking to him and even the third-stringers keeping their distance. He wondered whether his efforts to get back on the team were worth it considering the demoralizing environment around him. The team seemed to lack energy, as John watched from the sidelines as the first- and second-teams worked on offensive plays. Once they started scrimmaging, John noticed more sloppy play than usual. Coach Thompson caught an errant pass on the sideline and hurled the ball across the court.

"That's enough!" Coach shouted at those on the court. "This isn't good enough. Everybody's going to run until we start playing with some energy."

Junior forward Sam Stevens cracked up, trying to stifle his laughter.

"The beatings will continue until morale improves," Sam whispered.

A slight smile crossed John's face, trying not to laugh. The team lined up to run sprints as Coach Thompson lectured them about their efforts. John remained unsurprised when the team half-heartedly made their way up and down the court.

"We've got a game tomorrow, and I don't think you guys are ready!" Thompson bellowed to his unresponsive group. "What's wrong with you?"

After Coach Thompson realized more cardiovascular exercise may not cure what ailed the team, he sent the 10 players back onto the court to scrimmage for the last part of practice. After a few minutes, John made it on to the court with his teammates, who seemed eager to fire up shots. The quality of the shot did not seem to matter to most of the third group. After Sam forced up a shot into a triple team, missing badly, Coach Thompson replaced a couple players. John noticed that he hadn't put up a single shot during this entire scrimmage, making pass after pass, with none of them returning to him. He figured he better not worry about it since he may not need to shoot during a game anyway. As a teammate set a pick for John, starting guard Rashad Alexander threw an elbow that caught John in the ribs as he ran by. John bent over, stopping the scrimmage.

"Why are we stopping, guys?" Coach Thompson yelled from midcourt. "Let's go."

John glared at Rashad, who smiled at him.

John knew he shouldn't say anything, because the coach may blame him even if it wasn't his fault. John came off a pick and caught the ball, passing to Sam in the post. Stevens took a dribble toward the basket and found himself surrounded by three defenders. Instead of kicking back out to one of his open teammates, he tried forcing a shot and missed badly. John shook his head, looking over at his coach to see if he was watching. Coach Thompson did not react to the poor play, so John got back on defense. As practice ended, he had a hopeless feeling, wondering why he wanted to rejoin the team to begin with. As the players headed toward the locker room, John walked a short distance from Sam, who walked alongside fellow backups Erick Samuels, and Dan Zimmerman. Sam chatted loudly as always.

"Man, if I have to do anymore running, I may have to choose another sport."

"What, professional eating?" Erick responded.

"Keep shooting into triple teams, and you may get your wish," John muttered a few feet from the group.

"Shut up, John." Sam responded quickly. "You shouldn't even be on the team."

"At least I pass the ball once in a while. I didn't take a single shot all day, thanks to you forcing up a shot every time you could get your hands on the ball. That's why coach doesn't even yell at you anymore, and why you'll still be on the bench the rest of your high-school career. You should take this a little more seriously."

"You should talk, man," Zimmerman said defending his friend. "No one likes you, and you can't play."

"You're riding the pines too, Dan," John said. "All three of you played garbage basketball today, but it doesn't seem to bother you. At least I have the sense to not shoot while surrounded by three defenders."

The three guys glared at him, but John kept going. "I don't give a darn if you don't like me or if the starters cheap shot me every practice. I'm on the team, and I have nothing to lose by giving you a dose of reality. You guys act like you're perfect basketball players and never mess up, yet coach somehow doesn't play you. You should think about trying to improve. And why exactly are you giving me such a bad time? To stand up for a bunch of starters who don't like you? You turn against someone who never did anything to you, but now you won't even pass me the ball? That's pathetic."

John stormed into the locker room, throwing his shirt at the locker. His nose still hurt from the last time he pushed back against someone. John sat back against his locker as teammates made noise all around him.

"Hey John!" Rashad Alexander yelled to him from across the room. "How'd you like going against me today?"

John just wore a tired expression on his face as Rashad laughed and messed around with the starters. He glanced over at Braden, who had his back to him. He wondered how long these guys could keep it up.

"You gonna be getting that all season if you stick around that long," Rashad added.

"And if he does, it'll be at the end of the bench," Joe

Anthony added casually as he stood next to Rashad.

John shook his head and tried to pack his stuff as quickly as possible.

"Could things get any worse?" he wondered as he snuck out of the locker room. "Tomorrow's road game is not going to be fun."

The next morning John strolled to his locker in his basketball warm-up suit, which let the school know it was game day for the boys' basketball team. His shoulders slumped as he leaned against his locker, not wanting to participate in life on this cloudy Tuesday. From around the corner he heard what sounded like sobs coming from outside one of the classrooms. He walked a few steps and saw Braden's girlfriend Stephanie sitting on the floor outside a locked classroom with her hands on her face. Her elbows rested on her jeans, most of her face hidden from the few students who walked the halls twenty minutes before class.

"Everything OK?" John said hesitantly, not sure if he wanted to intervene.

Stephanie looked up at him, trying to figure out who was talking to her and why.

"John?"

John put his back to the wall and let himself slide to the floor within a few feet of her.

"Where's Braden?"

"Still sleeping, probably," Stephanie said somewhat bitterly. "We had a fight last night, and I think things might be over."

"I'm sorry."

"Yeah, sure you are."

"I don't hate Braden. I just don't like the way he's been acting since he became a starter and began acting differently."

"You didn't have to take a cheap shot at him."

"I know I didn't, I screwed up. I was mad, it was at the end of a frustrating practice. I don't know what more to say, it was a heat-of-the-moment thing. So why are you defending him if you're fighting with him?"

"That's not the reason I'm upset. My parents are divorcing."

"Oh, I'm sorry. That's rough."

"Yeah."

"Have things been bad for a while?"

"They're always fighting. My dad makes a lot of money but works all the time. My mom works too but doesn't make as much. I don't know what will happen once he's gone."

"You have siblings?"

"A brother in eighth grade. He's been torn up about this. He plays a lot of video games and pretends to hold it together, but I know he's upset."

John stared ahead and didn't talk for a bit.

"I don't know what to say, I can't imagine that. My parents are a little boring and not always a fan of me playing basketball, but no fighting or anything. I guess I have it pretty good in that regard."

"Why do you want to talk to me about this?"

"I told you, I don't hate Braden or anybody. I heard you crying. My locker's right there, so I wanted to see what's up. I'm sorry about all this. I know there's nothing I can say to make you feel better. Just give it time I guess. Things will work out OK. You'll be off to college next year and can do whatever you want."

"Yeah. You're a good listener, John."

"Thanks. I hope things work out for you and Braden. He may come around."

"He doesn't listen to me and just wants to hang out with his teammates now that we've been dating for a short time. He wants to spend more time with them than me."

John nodded. "Braden and I were best friends for years, but

then he worked his way into the starting lineup and wanted to hang out with the big shots instead of a benchwarmer. He seemed to get an attitude and thought he had it made with a girlfriend and everything. Maybe he'll get over it, maybe he won't."

"So you're not really that evil, are you?" Stephanie said with a slight smile.

"Nah, at least I don't think so," John replied with a grin. "Braden's buddies and the guys on the bench are making my life miserable since I came back onto the team, though. I don't know how much more I can take. They know if I fight back, I'll take the blame and be kicked off the team, which is what they want. To stay on the team, I have to take their crap and they know it. I'm in a losing battle. I just hope they lose interest in me after a while."

"Do you think I should stay with Braden?"

John laughed. "Not my call. I don't know if he'll change or not. I wouldn't have been friends with him if he wasn't a somewhat decent guy. Stuff just went to his head. I don't think his new friends are a good influence, but he's going to stay friends with them."

John sat with Stephanie for another minute before the first bell rang. As they got up, Braden appeared with a frown on his face.

"What are you doing with my girl, John?"

"How do I know you're the owner of this girl, Braden? You'll have to produce some papers first."

Stephanie cracked up next to him.

"Shut up, John!" Braden yelled as he shoved him up against the wall.

"Yeah, I've been getting a lot of that lately," John snapped back.

He looked at Braden with a frown.

"Kind of ironic, huh?" John said, putting up his hands, signaling he didn't want to fight. "Everybody's ticked at me for being aggressive and you're kind of doing the same thing right now. Maybe the reason you and some others are giving me such a bad time isn't all because of that but because you guys are jerks and need to give someone a bad time."

"You ever come near my girl again and I'll drop you in a second."

John looked to Stephanie. "Forget what I said, I'm not sure he's worth it."

"What did he say to you?" Braden glared at Stephanie.

"I can talk to who I want. He actually didn't tell me to drop you, even though I realize I should. John's a lot better dude than you are. And by the way, you don't own me."

With that, Stephanie stormed off. John looked at Braden with a cold stare. "At least you have your fake basketball friends, right? Funny thing is, I didn't see them hanging with you before you cracked the starting lineup. But now it's fun to be one of them and ditch everyone else, right?"

"Whatever, you just want what I have?"

"Which is what exactly? What'll you have when basketball is done?"

"I've got a lot of basketball left."

"Keep dreaming," John laughed. "I'd be doing just fine if you and your buddies weren't such jerks all the time. If you think this is about jealousy, you just don't get it. You've changed and too many guys on the team are full of themselves."

Braden turned to walk away. "Enjoy life at the end of the bench tonight."

As it turned out, John sitting on the end of the bench that evening may have been the best place. The Leopards began with an uninspiring start at home against Central High, the second-to-last place team in the conference standings. The starters struggled, turning the ball over as their coach winced from the sideline. Braden was at the heart of the team's issues, missing shots and committing turnovers. John noticed the team looked like it did in practice yesterday, lacking energy and focus. John put negative thoughts out of his mind, trying not to be happy his tormenters had problems. With the score tied at 34 at halftime, John could tell Coach Thompson would soon launch into one of his famed halftime tirades. Coach did not let him down, starting to yell before the team could find their seats.

"You guys better pick it up, right now!" Coach Thompson bellowed, glaring at his starters. "I don't see any energy out there tonight, and we're playing a team we should have put away already. What's wrong with all of you?"

Most of the guys wore a blank stare on their faces, not wanting to offer explanations and certainly not wanting to challenge their angry coach.

"If you don't pick it up, I'll send the next five in who maybe will play with some energy," Coach Thompson continued.

"Whoa, hold on coach," John whispered to his bench mates with a smirk on his face. "Let's not get carries away. That's crazy talk!"

John knew he heard that one before, but wondered if the coach was capable of such a move. John decided he was bluffing, and the starters probably recognized this. John figured those at the end of the bench would not get in unless the game became a blowout with less than two minutes remaining. Just three backups played in the first half, and John figured no one else would play.

The second half featured a poor effort by North. The Leopards managed a 10-point advantage by the end of the third quarter at 55-45, but did not look better than they did in the first half. John sat next to junior guard Terrance White at the end of the bench, who chatted with fellow backups Juan Hernandez and Erick Samuels. Terrance complained about the starters, but John remembered his fellow benchwarmers' own poor efforts in yesterday's practice. John thought about chatting with his teammates but decided against it, not wanting the night to get worse. North held onto the 10-point advantage and won by that margin. As John figured, only eight guys saw action that evening despite a lackluster showing from Braden and company. The team still had just one loss on the season but was not playing its best basketball.

As John strolled through the door of his home later that night, he saw the living room light aglow, with his parents sitting in their chairs reading.

"Hey John, how was the game?" his mother asked, looking up from her magazine.

"We won," John responded half-heartedly.

"Yeah, did you get in?" his father asked.

"Nope, if I get in a game the rest of the year I'll be lucky."

His parents went back to reading. John knew basketball was not their thing, and rarely took interest in his sport. As he headed to his bedroom, he checked his phone and saw Amber left a message. He returned the call, looking forward to chatting with her.

"Hey Amber, how are you?"

"Hi John, how did the game go?"

"Well, you know, we won but didn't do too well. We're at 13-1 on the season now."

"When's your next game?"

"Thursday at Riverfront and then we play again on Friday at home against Kennedy High. You coming out to any of them? I can hold down a bench like no one else in the history of mankind!"

Amber laughed. "Yeah, I think Courtney and I will go to the home one. I've got some studying left tonight, but I'll talk to you tomorrow."

"Yeah, good talking to you, it's going to be a long day of practice tomorrow. An angry coach and uninspired players. A great combination."

As John walked to his locker the next morning, he saw Stephanie again who flashed him an awkward smile.

"Hey John."

"Stephanie, how are you?"

She nodded. "Braden didn't go crazy on you, did he?"

"No. You feeling any better?"

"Not really. I just wish things would get better. Braden's mad at me for talking to you."

"Yeah, why did you do that, anyway?" John asked with a smile. "I can't even get my own teammates to talk to me, and you're the one person I'm not supposed to talk to."

"You listened to me. My friends have parents who are still together and they don't want to hear about my life. I don't think Braden does, either."

"Sorry to hear that."

"So how's basketball going?"

"You mean other than the fact that no one will talk to me because of one stupid mistake? Yeah, I'm not sure why I decided to get back on the team. The coach yells at us all the time, the players don't seem to care and I get hit with cheap shots in practice. And of course I sit on my butt at the end of the bench on game days. So yeah, I'm still trying to figure out whether I'm happy being back on the team."

"Sounds rough."

"It'll be OK, just a couple of months left in the season."

"So what do you think I should do with my family problems?"

"Well, based on my mistakes, try not to get angry with anyone. You want to be a good role model for your brother. He's going to have maybe a rougher time than you with this. And I'm sure your mom will need your help. You're a nice person, you have a lot to offer them. Hey, I wanted to ask you something."

"Yeah, shoot."

"When we first met, you didn't say much to me. What was up with that? You girls were kind of glued to your phones and gossiping about others."

Stephanie smiled. "Yeah, that's what my group does. I know it's stupid."

"But you wouldn't want someone bashing you behind your back, right?"

She smiled a bit wider. "You're probably right. It's just hard not to."

John smiled back. "Everybody needs friends, so I guess we should be as nice as we can to others. I'm not sure how that will work, since it doesn't seem to be working on my basketball team. And then I get mad at them and say stuff that ticks them off."

"I just wish my parents wouldn't yell so much in front of us. I wish there was something I could do."

"It's their fault, not yours. You can't make them happy, this is between them. Just take care of your brother and you'll be ready to move out next fall."

"Yeah, thanks."

That afternoon, the team continued its listless play. John tried to take advantage of the limited time he got on the floor, but became frustrated with himself after a couple of his passes ended up in the hands of the defense. John dribbled down the court and saw what he thought was an open teammate. He tossed the pass, but Rashad Alexander knocked the pass back toward John. Both guys hustled toward the ball and dove for it. John and Rashad both got their arms around the ball, but Rashad delivered an elbow to John's ribs that forced a grunt from him. He let go of the ball as Coach Thompson awarded the ball to Rashad's group. John glared at Rashad, who began talking trash to him.

On the ride home, John once again felt helpless about his situation. He thought about going through the remainder of the season hated and rotting on the end of the pines. Coach hadn't said much to him since he rejoined the team, and he felt invisible. That evening, John chatted with Amber on the phone.

"John, you seem distracted," Amber said at the end of the service.

"Yeah, I'm sorry. I had a tough basketball practice. Things are kind of tough. I think I need to practice more or something. I'm gonna go to the YMCA tonight and shoot."

"Don't you have studying to do?"

"Yeah, I'll get it done, it just may be a late night."

John wanted to do things differently this time. He knew he should put in work on his own, otherwise he would not get better from a few minutes of scrimmage time each day. John worked on his ball handling and shooting, listening to the sounds of his basketball bounce on the court, since he had the YMCA court to himself this late at night. The workout also helped him relax from the pressures that seemed to weigh him down no matter what he did. His teammates disliked him, he got punched by a bully that he feared was not done with him and he still did not know what he wanted to do after this year. He hoped it would all work out, but he had a feeling it was going to be a long ride until graduation.

The next morning John made his way from his locker to Ambers before class but met eyes with Coach Thompson on his way.

"Hey John," Coach said, stopping in the hall.

"Hi Coach."

"We haven't had much of a chance to chat since you rejoined the team, have we?"

"Uh, no sir."

"How are things going?"

John took a deep breath, not knowing how to answer. He wasn't sure whether honesty is the best policy or not.

"I appreciate being back on the team, but it's been a little rough."

"Yeah, how so?"

"My teammates won't talk to me, and I keep taking cheap shots in practice, to be honest."

"Mmmm. Have you tried to talk with everyone?"

"Yeah, they won't have it. They want me off the team and just haven't warmed up to being friendly with me like before. I don't know what to do other than keep trying."

"Well, just be patient I guess. I have to run, but we'll talk more sometime."

John appreciated the coach talking to him, but realized he didn't say anything about the cheap shots. He'd rather those stop than teammates talk to him.

As John started to walk, Amber came up to him from her locker a few feet away.

"Hey, I saw you talking to coach Thompson."

"Yeah, he just wanted to chat. I mentioned a couple of the problems I've had since I rejoined the team."

"That's good. By the way, I talked to Courtney and we'll go to your home game Friday."

"Cool, it will be good to have you there. Maybe you can sit next to me on the end of the bench and see if anyone notices."

Amber giggled. "I think someone might, at least the other

95

guys sitting there."

"We'd actually probably like that. You could bring us pizza if we get hungry, and coach couldn't get mad at you for leaving the bench."

"Hey, I won't be running errands for you guys!"

"OK, I guess that's asking too much."

That evening, John rode the bus to the away game at Riverfront, in third place behind North and West. The Leopards wanted to avenge their home loss to the team a couple games ago. He knew if the team didn't play better, this could be a rough night. After the first couple of possessions, the Leopards confirmed John's suspicions. The players lacked energy once again, turning the ball over and letting Riverfront get easy looks at the basket. Coach Thompson looked as red in the face as he did at yesterday's practice. Near the end of the half, he put in all five second-stringers.

"Put me in coach," Terrance said softly as not to alert the coach to his demands.

John shook his head to himself, remembering how poorly he played in practice yesterday.

"I wouldn't count on it, man."

"Who asked you?" Terrance shot back at John.

"Hey John, can you get me some water?" Erick Samuels said, looking past Terrance. "I'm dying of thirst here."

"I didn't know you could get winded watching others burn calories."

John looked back at Terrance. "It's not my problem coach is playing Juan instead of you. Stop turning the ball over in practice if you want to play. At least I know why I'm sitting here."

"Why? Because you're a screw up?" Terrance remarked.

"You guys mess up, and you'll find that out soon enough, so get over yourselves."

The two teammates raised their eyebrows at John's harsh words.

"You know guys, I'd really like to be on good terms with you. I wish you would just let it go and treat me like anyone else. It's not like you guys were buds with Braden anyway. If you can't let it go, it's going to stink, because we're going to be on the bench together for quite a few more games here."

"Why should we?" Erick asked.

"Didn't I just say why? It's not like I was a jerk to you before I got in trouble, and I don't have anything against you guys other than how poorly we're playing in practice."

As John finished his sentence, the halftime buzzer sounded, with North trailing by eight points. The five starters finished the half sitting next to John and the two unlucky souls remaining on the bench. Coach Thompson generated another halftime tirade, letting the team know that unless they picked up their effort, they may not win another game all season. John wondered the effectiveness of these outbursts as the team continued to play poorly in the second half.

"What are we doing out there?" Juan Hernandez asked from the bench.

"It's not like we practiced well the last few times," John remarked to a silent audience.

North tried to rally in the fourth quarter when their deficit ballooned to 14 points, but it was not enough, as Riverfront won by six points. The bus ride home was a silent one after Coach Thompson expressed his frustration in the locker room after the game, losing to Riverfront twice in the last three games. He was thankful those installing the locker room benches secured them to the floor for fear of Coach Thompson throwing one of them.

"What happened last night?" Amber asked John the following morning on the way to class.

"We haven't been playing well the last few nights, including practices," John explained. "You don't practice well, you probably don't play well in games. Just like in choir, right?"

Amber smiled. "Why isn't the team doing well? They had been playing well until then?"

"No one has much energy in practice. I'm not sure what's up. Maybe it goes back to my frustrations earlier in the year. Players don't like each other. Starters only hang out with starters, backups with backups. It's not a real fun team to be around lately."

"Sounds like it," Amber relied empathetically. "Should I still come out to the game tonight with Courtney."

"Yeah, why not? We're playing Kennedy High, a team that isn't good. If we can't win that one, we will be in trouble the rest of the year."

Kennedy High stood as the second-worst team in the conference and played like it that night. The home crowd seemed to give the Leopards a bit more energy, as they jumped out to a 20-7 lead at the end of the first quarter. By halftime, North built a 43-15 lead.

Terrance White sat next to John rubbing his hands shortly into the third quarter.

"Looks like we'll be getting in!" he said in anticipation. "I can't wait to show the crowd what I got tonight."

"Hey, does my hair look good?" Sam Stevens remarked, three seats from where John sat. "Somebody told me my hair looked like a toupee the other day."

"Jealousy drives people to say crazy things," Erick Samuels remarked, brushing his own red hair. "See those three girls up there? Those will be my dates at the end of the night when I put it down."

"Put it down?" Terrance replied. "You mean a

cheeseburger? You ain't never dunked in your life."

John looked up at the stands and saw Courtney and Amber on the bleachers on the other side of the court. He glanced over the crowd, and noticed Stephanie with her friends. She didn't look too happy, despite the chatter of her friends in between examining their phones. He also noticed Matt hanging out with his shady friends near the top of the bleachers. He wondered how his friend Steve would do the rest of the year, coping with those guys. John's jabbering teammates and the sounding of the buzzer signaling the end of the third quarter brought him back into the moment.

The scoreboard read 67-30, signaling to everyone on the bench to ready themselves for game action.

Junior guard Dominique Carter leaned over to those on the bench to his right shortly into the fourth quarter. "Hey, guys!" he said in a loud whisper.

The six guys to his right looked over at him.

"You down for tomorrow night?"

Junior forward Dan Zimmerman looked at him. "What's Saturday night?"

"You better not have plans. Big party at Damon's house Saturday night. Usual story, his parents are out of town for the weekend and leaving their two-story place in his care. You know."

"Damon? Who's Damon?" Sam wondered.

"He's a senior dude on the tennis team," Dominique explained. "Anyway, starts at nine. Important thing is, there are going to be girls and liquor. You in?"

Chapter 7

John shook his head, stunned by his teammates' willingness to consider reckless behavior in the middle of basketball season.

"I don't know," Erick responded to Dominique. "What if we get busted or something?"

"Oh, come on," Dominique responded. "Damon's paying off the neighbors, dude. And it's winter. No one's going to be hanging out in the yard. Besides, it's an exclusive party. No losers invited, so that means you, John!"

"Thanks, Dominique, I appreciate that," John said, smiling back. He looked at his teammates. "You all hate me anyway, so I'll say it. You guys are idiots if you go, you know that, right? Anyone finds out, you'll all be off the team and the season will get cancelled or something. Coach won't put up with that."

Rashad looked over at the group. "Don't worry guys, you won't have to worry about any of this, because none of ya'll are invited. Starters only. You guys can sit at home like you always do."

The guys next to John grew silent until Erick spoke.

"Thanks Rashad, you're so welcoming."

John chuckled. "Then I guess it's settled. You guys would have been idiots to go to that, anyway."

"I hate to agree with the loser, but he's right," Sam said to Dominique. "It was too big a risk. Besides, I'll have all the girls I need after I do that windmill dunk tonight."

"Now it's a windmill?" Terrance questioned. "Dude if you

touch the net you should be happy."

As he said that, Coach Thompson started calling out names to go in. After a few minutes of the second-string playing, he looked over once again. "Erick. Terrance. Let's go, get over to the scorer's table."

A big space on the bench now existed between John and the starting five, the only others on the bench at the moment, as Erick and Terrance went to replace Darnell Jackson and Dan Zimmerman on the court. John wondered if he may eventually get in, but he did not expect to play. The backups fared predictably, as sloppy play and a couple wild shots defined the final five minutes. The crowd roared as Juan Gonzalez hit a jumper and Sam Stevens scored on a put back off a missed shot. John shook his head as Erick and Terrance threw up wild shots in an effort to notch points but to no avail.

As the clocked ticked down, John felt a wide range of emotions, including embarrassment, frustration and confusion. He looked up at the lights, trying to get a grip.

"Deep breaths," John told himself. "It will all be OK."

John remembered the words of his parents saying that basketball is not that important. He knew at that moment he had a choice to make.

"Should I get frustrated or not worry about it?" John asked himself.

He wondered what Coach Thompson may be thinking with his decision to hold him out of the game. John questioned whether coach made the decision to make an example of him. Maybe he only wanted to test John to see his reaction to this disappointment. John knew coach would likely never give him an answer, so all he could do is make the best of it if he wanted to stay on the team. He lost his spot on the team before, and he did not want lose it again. The final buzzer sounded with the score of 82-50. John shook hands with his opponents and quickly made his way to the locker room. He dressed quickly and headed back toward the gym as several of the starters, including Braden, Rashad Alexander and Teyshaun White first entered the locker room.

"Did you enjoy your playing time, John?" Teyshaun asked John mockingly.

Rashad laughed as he walked by. John did not respond and glared at Braden as he kept walking.

"Why on earth do I want to be on a basketball team?" John wondered to himself as he walked down the empty school hallway. He went to the gym to meet Amber and Courtney, wondering what they would say after seeing him sitting out a game in which he could have played.

"Hey John," Amber said with a smile on her face, greeting him as he made his way into the gym where fans mingled.

"You must have had to take a shower after all that action tonight," Courtney said, smiling.

John rolled his eyes. "Yeah, of course."

"What's up with that? You were, like, the only one who didn't get in?" Amber asked.

"I don't know. Can't read coach's mind. I'll just keep plugging away and we'll see what happens in future games."

"So what's going on this weekend, you want to do something?" Courtney asked Amber and John.

"Yeah, we could do something," John replied. "I'm going to have to work out at the YMCA a couple of times to keep my basketball game sharp so I'm ready if I ever get in a game, but I have plenty of time to do something."

"Yeah, I can make it work," Amber added.

"You bringing Steve again?" Courtney said with a smile.

"I don't know," John said. "It was kind of a one-time thing. I think he enjoyed it, but he'll have to make some friends of his own age at some point. We won't be here to hang with him next year. Courtney, you could bring our friend Matt along!"

"Shut up!" Courtney said, half laughing. "He would beat you up again and the night would be over."

"Hey, I could have taken him if I wanted to be violent," John said defensively with a grin. "You two would make a great pair. It might be a somewhat volatile relationship, however."

As the group talked, a familiar voice called out to John.

"Hey All-Star, how are you?" Don Harmon said to John, as Julie strode up to the group alongside her husband.

"Hey you two, thanks for coming out to the game," John said.

"Hang in there, you'll get your chance," Don said, understanding how John might be feeling at the moment.

"If I was, this would have been the night," John responded quietly.

Saturday afternoon, John mingled with the many other hoopsters at the local YMCA. The Midwest winter brought people looking for something to do into the large building this time of year. John worked on the usual skills his coach told him to improve while trying to push the thoughts out of his head that he may never see game action. He was happy his parents had another obligation that night, so he didn't have to explain why he was wasting his time on a fruitless activity. John put in a couple of hours until he was sore, knowing he may need to be sharp in practice in order to play his best. With his frustration about not getting into the game the previous evening, he nearly forgot about the party his teammates may be attending.

"Would some team members really be stupid enough to do something like that near the end of the basketball season?" John wondered to himself.

He knew some of them might be.

"Peer pressure is a wonderful thing," John thought.

The group planned to go to a movie and a restaurant that preferably did not contain Matt the bully. John thought that he should ask Matt his food preferences beforehand, so he knew what restaurants to avoid.

As John made his way toward Amber's house later that evening, he saw headlights pulling into a large home in a nice subdivision down the road. At least 10 cards adorned the house, with more pulling in. John took a left turn, instead of continuing toward Amber's house. John pulled over to the side of the street, far enough from the other cars but close enough to investigate. He waited for the drivers of the cars that just pulled in to leave their vehicle on this chilly evening to see who they were. John checked his car clock to make sure he had time to make a short investigation before stopping at Amber's house. He had a few minutes to spare, so he continued observing the situation at hand. A couple of seniors exited their respective vehicles, each with a paper bag. John shook his head as they approached the door, which opened.

"I'll bet that's Damon!" John said comically to himself, as the two teens entered the home, which stood aglow.

"Shoot, I better get out of here," John said as he realized he needed to get to Amber's house on time.

John did a U-turn to speed the process of picking up his date and made his way a few blocks to Amber's abode. John texted her from the driveway, alerting her to his arrival.

"Hey John!" Amber said, jumping into the passenger seat.

"Hey, how are you?" John asked. "How would you like to make a brief pit stop before picking up Courtney?"

Amber looked at him, trying to figure out if John's tone hinted at any mischief.

"Did you want to pull over and make out or something?"

She asked, laughing.

"I had something else in mind, but that could work too," John responded. "Just don't tell my parents. No, I, uh, stumbled upon something that might interest you just a couple of blocks away."

"Ah, do I sense some mystery from you?" Amber replied.

"Definitely, I thought we could do a bit of detective work before picking up Courtney. Can you text her and ask if it would be OK if we were a bit late?"

"Sure."

"Hopefully she doesn't get mad for missing out, but I'm too curious to wait any longer."

Amber typed away on her screen as John pulled out of the driveway, heading back to where the action will take place. John took a right to toward the house, as Amber looked out her side window.

"You're right, this is close by," Amber commented, looking down the road.

"So what I forgot to tell you last night is that my awesome teammates discussed attending a party. Only starters were invited, however, despite most of my teammates wanting to go. The backups told me I wasn't invited, because I'm a 'loser' but then one of our starters told them they can't go either."

"You gonna call the cops on them?" Amber asked as John pulled over to the side of the road as he did before.

John laughed. "No, they should get busted the normal way. You know, too much noise, kids stumbling out into the yard, the neighborhood busybody calls the police. You know how it works."

"That sounds about right."

"What I want to know is, who's in and who's out of this operation," John said humorously. "I want to know names and I want them right now."

"Let's drive past the cars and circle around, see if we recognize any vehicles."

"Sure thing."

John pulled out onto the road and slowly began driving past the other cars toward the party house. The host had every light on in the two-story home, making the residence in this otherwise silent neighborhood this Saturday evening look conspicuous.

"Maybe we're jumping to conclusions," John said. "I'm sure they're all just having a board game night."

"Or using the board games as coasters for their beer," Amber added.

"That's a more likely scenario."

At that moment, John took a long look to his left as he passed several cars.

"Umm, that's Braden's vehicle," John stated.

"Seriously? What's wrong with him? Doesn't he know he could get in big time trouble for this?"

"Well, Braden wants a life of superstardom. He seems to care about one thing – himself. He just wants to hang with his fellow starters and have fun. I doubt he considered anything bad happening."

"I guess you're right."

"I told my teammates who were on the bench with me at the time last night to stay the heck away, and I would guess they will since they were told not to go by the starters. Some of the backups don't really hang with the prima donnas anyway. Not sure about the starters, though. I'm sure a couple starters talked Braden into going. He wants to fit in, and we all have to fit in, don't we?"

Amber nodded as John passed the last of the cars lined along the city street and pulled over once again. John stared straight ahead looking into the darkness straight ahead. "You know, Braden was my best friend since elementary school and we played basketball and hung out together all these years. Once we got to varsity, he started getting more playing time and all of a sudden things changed. It wouldn't have been so bad if his fellow superstars were good guys, but they're not. They look down on those who aren't blessed with their supposed gifts. I guess Braden will have to figure all that out for himself."

"So do you think he'll drop out of college or something?"

"No, he'll do OK. He's a smart guy and will get through school. Maybe he can get one of those Wall Street jobs where you make a lot of money but don't have a conscience."

"What are the chances your teammates get busted for this?"

"I don't even care at this point. They're wasting their basketball season and just going through the motions. Nothing I can do about it other than push them in practice, but coach won't care. He'll just yell at them more if they start losing more games."

"Well, I guess we better pick Courtney up, huh?"

John looked at the clock. "Yeah, I guess. We'll still have time to catch the movie. Mind if I do this first, though?"

With that, John leaned over and gave Amber a kiss.

"Wow, that was pretty smooth, John," Amber said, smiling.

"Thanks, I have skills."

"From lots of practice?"

"No, of course not!" John replied, mocking defensiveness.

Amber frowned, pretending to question him.

"I mean, those three girls forced me to make out with them. They threatened me. If I didn't, they would have told everyone I listen to boy bands. I had no choice."

Courtney hopped into the backseat a few minutes later.

"So, did I miss anything?"

Amber gave John a mischievous smile.

"Oh, not too much," John replied, winking at Amber.

"Wait, what's going on?" Courtney said, looking at both of them in the front seat.

"You're missing the party of the century right now," John said.

"What? Where?"

"Over at some kid named Damon's house, near Amber's home."

"You want to go there instead?" Amber said, looking back on Courtney.

"Maybe, that sounds more exciting than a movie."

"Oh, it will be, especially when the police show up and you have to make a run for it while trying to escape the house and not tripping over empty booze bottles," John joked.

"So who's all there?" Courtney enquired.

"I'm pretty sure the starting lineup for the basketball team," John explained. "No word if they needed the cheerleaders encouraging them up while they have they succeed taking a different type of shot."

The trio made it to the movie just in time. As they exited the theatre a couple hours later, they debated whether to eat something or scope out the party.

"I'm pretty sure they'll still be at it by the time we're done eating," John said, trying to persuade Courtney. "I'm starving."

"You already got to check the party out, I want to see for myself."

"I'm with John," Amber replied. "I'm hungry, and they'll still be going strong when we're done."

"It's not like somebody will stand at the top of the stairs yelling to everyone 'Hey guys, it's 10 p.m., we should be getting home so we can get some sleep!' Besides, from what I heard from my teammates, the hosts' parents are gone all weekend so he'll have plenty of time to clean up." John stated.

"Alright, let's get some crappy fast food," Courtney said, realizing she was outnumbered.

"Hey, I like fast food," John replied. "I'm not one of those fancy guys who needs to eat at a country club or something."

"I don't think high-schoolers eat at country clubs anyway," Amber said jokingly.

"Just wherever you go, make sure your buddy Matt and the gang aren't there," Courtney reminded John.

"I'm with you on that," John agreed.

As the three munched on burgers a few minutes later, Courtney wanted details about the shenanigans going on at the now-legendary Damon's home.

"So how did this Damon guy pull this off?" Courtney wondered.

John looked seriously at her. "Please don't refer to him as simply Damon. He deserves more respect than that. Please call him Damon the Great. You see, Courtney, few students have the mental capacity to coordinate such an effort. It takes timing, waiting for that rare opportunity when parents leave for an entire weekend. Once that moment occurs, a coordinated effort must begin immediately to invite throngs of alcohol-obsessed, rule-breaking teens over to his perfectly empty home. A successful marketing campaign must begin."

"So what happens if a parent catches wind on social media of this event?" Courtney said, grinning.

"That's what makes Damon so great, he clearly pulled it off. At least until his parents notice something amiss upon their arrival."

Courtney's grin widened. "What if he has parents who are there partying with their son?"

"That wouldn't be the first time that's happened, but like I said, it sounded like this was an adult-free event. I just hope he knows how to clean up a mess."

Courtney looked at John and Amber anxiously. "You guys ready to go? I want to check this out, and I can't be out too late or my parents will get after me."

John answered first. "Yeah, alright. Let's go."

As John pulled into the neighborhood, he immediately saw the cars lined down the street and shook his head.

"Yeah, like they're not going to get caught," John remarked. "Cars are everywhere. Damon couldn't have paid off that many people."

"Wow!" Courtney exclaimed. "This is a party."

"Some bad NBA teams could only hope for a turnout like this at their arena!" John added.

"Pull up to the house, let's see if we know anyone here," Courtney prodded John.

"OK, OK."

Amber rolled down her window as they approached the home, listening to music booming outside the residence.

"I can't see anyone from here, they have the front blinds down," Courtney complained. "Wait, the one window on the side is open. I have to go in."

"Seriously?" Amber asked. "Why? Do you want to get in trouble like everyone in the house?"

"No, I just want to take a peek in the window and then I'll be right back," Courtney explained.

"What if the police come?" Amber questioned.

"Oh, they won't arrive in the time it takes for me to do this. John, pull over."

John passed the last of the cars and pulled over. "Alright, but I'm peeling out of here if I see law enforcement officials. And I will tell them you are partying harder than anyone!"

"Yeah, you do that. I'll be back in a minute."

With that, Courtney jumped out of the passenger seat and

ran toward the house, which was a good distance from where John parked. He looked in the rear view mirror as Courtney jogged past car after car on the sidewalk. John smiled as he realized she must go through a bit of snow to get to the window.

"She's up to no good," John said, mocking exasperation. "Wait until the police find her footprints in the backyard."

"Well if she's up to no good, maybe I should be up to no good," Amber replied as she leaned over to kiss John.

"Very nice," John replied. "Practice makes perfect. That was a nice move there, young lady."

"Hey, I learned from you, right?"

"I am a smooth operator. You have to watch out for those kind of people, they usually are players. I only play basketball and not well."

John looked in his rear-view mirror to see if Courtney would reappear after her investigation. After a few minutes, they spotted her running toward the car. She hopped in, out of breath.

"Alright, I looked in the window and saw a ton of people in there," Courtney muttered in between deep breaths.

"Anyone we know?" John asked casually.

"Yeah, I think there were some basketball guys there, a bunch of senior girls. A lot of drinking going on. I saw a whole table of liquor in the kitchen."

"How much could you see through one window?" Amber asked.

"It was the kitchen window. That's where people were getting drinks from, and I could see into the living room, too. That's one big party."

"Geez, there are gonna be some hung over kids and angry parents tomorrow," John added.

As the three friends talked, they began hearing what

sounded to be the faint sound of sirens from behind them.

"Time to go," John said, pulling the car onto the street.

"Wait, let's drive around a bit and then come back in a few minutes," Amber explained. "Once the cops arrive, we'll just drive by to see what's up."

"Good idea," John said. "I'm too curious to just leave and go home. Even if we get stopped, they'll see we haven't been drinking."

"Let's go to my place and hang out a bit," Amber said.

"Oh, John will get to meet Amber's parents, huh?" Courtney said, trying to get a rise out of John.

"Do they know you're friends with Amber?" John asked. "If so, maybe they'll be hesitant to let their impressionable young daughter hang out with someone who peeps in on wild parties."

"They know I'm a troublemaker."

John entered Amber's house tentatively. He saw her parents at church, but had never met them.

Amber greeted her parents as she came in and introduced John. Her mother, who wore short red hair and looked to be around 50 years old, stuck out her hand.

"Hi John, nice to meet you. I'm Lori. Amber mentioned you're one of her new friends."

"Hi," John replied, reaching out to shake her hand. "Yeah, we've been in the same class for years and at the same church obviously, but we became friends recently."

Amber's father, a rather large man with dark wavy hair got up from his recliner and walked over to John.

"Hi John, I'm Arthur. I'm used to seeing Courtney here, so this is unusual to have more than one person over."

"I hope it doesn't throw things off," John replied. "I'm glad she was willing to take on one more friend."

"So, you watching the Super Bowl this weekend, John?"

Arthur asked him.

John felt relieved he seemed like a normal guy and not one who wanted to show him his belt buckle collection or something.

"Yeah, of course. I watch plenty of football, and this is the biggest weekend of them all, right? I was going to ask the girls if they wanted to come over to our house for the Super Bowl on Sunday, actually."

"Well, we don't have any plans, so I don't see why not," Lori chipped in.

"Yeah, I could do that," Amber replied. "What do you think, Courtney?"

"I can make that work. I hope you have good food."

John chuckled. "My mom will probably make something that's decent. We always had Braden over every year, so my family is used to hosting."

"He's not coming over this year?" Courtney asked, knowing the answer.

"Yeah, probably not," John replied. "He may have a few issues to deal with this weekend."

"Yeah, I was going to tell you that a huge party is going on just a couple blocks away," Amber said to her parents. "We drove by, and tons of high schoolers were there. As we left, we heard police sirens. We're heading back in a few minutes to see if people are in trouble."

"Wow," Lori said. "So your classmates are going to be in trouble, huh?"

"Yeah, John's teammates may have some explaining to do," Courtney added.

"Let's just hope party pictures don't get posted online, otherwise they may be in bigger trouble," John explained and then changed the subject. "So, Amber tells me you're a nurse and your husband works for a technology company?"

"Yes," Lori said with a smile. "I've worked at the hospital in town for over 20 years.

"Nice," John said, noticing their house was similar to his parents' home. The residence was old but well-kept.

"John, it was nice to finally meet you, and Courtney, always good to see you," Arthur said with a smile as the three friends walked toward the door.

"Yeah, it was nice meeting you," John said.

As they headed into the cold, Courtney tried getting a rise out of John.

"So, John, how did you like meeting your future in-laws?"

"Shut up, Courtney," Amber said.

"Really, Courtney, what are we, in eighth grade?" John fired back. "I have to say, Amber, you have a nice house. It's, like, similar to mine."

"Thanks I guess. It's from the 50s, so it's a bit old."

"My parents' house is kind of old, like, from the same era. We keep in clean, though, which I think counts for something."

"Well that's good to know," Courtney said. "You don't have empty bottles and newspapers laying all over?"

"No, but that's what would happen if my parents weren't neat. My dad reads lots of newspapers. I think he only reads the boring ones, though, because he never has great stories. Never once has he said, 'Hey, did you hear the story of the cannibal that ate the clown and thought he tasted funny?'"

"That's awful," Amber said.

Courtney laughed. "That would be a stupid news story anyway."

"At least it would be interesting, as opposed to interest rates in Switzerland," John explained. "Don't they make good watches or something?"

"I think so," Courtney said. "Or maybe it's chocolate."

"How about chocolate watches?" Amber said.

"In Missouri you can still wear those for nine months out of the year without them melting," John said with a smile. "Moving on from cannibals and chocolate watches, what do you two want to do when we get there?"

"Wait, I wanted to hear more about Swiss interest rates," Courtney said. "Anyway, let's just play it by ear and see what's going on there first."

"Good idea," John added.

John reached the party street within a couple minutes and immediately noticed flashing red, white and blue lights, accompanied by sirens.

"Busted," John remarked.

Several squad cars double parked alongside the cars already lined along the street.

Courtney put her head out the window despite the cold to see the action. "Wow, this is crazy! Monday is going to be interesting at school for sure. John, drive by so we can see if cops are talking to students."

"Alright, I want to see this too," John said, driving ahead. "As long as I have enough room to make it between the double parked cars. Hitting a cop car would probably be bad, so I'll drive slowly."

John drove past the police cars slowly and then came to a brief stop as he made it to the house full of partiers.

"You gonna get out to investigate once again, Courtney?" John asked, hoping she's say no this time.

"No, I don't think so," Courtney responded. "No way I'm getting mixed up in this."

"Why? Your mug shot would look great on the front page of our local newspaper, especially since you're no longer a juvenile, right?" John ribbed her.

"So how many people do you think will get busted?"

Amber asked.

"Those who aren't fast enough to escape," John said wryly.

John looked to his right and saw officers taking names and making sure no one left the scene. As he drove past, he saw Braden's vehicle still sitting on the side of the road.

"Well, this should make for an interesting Monday morning," he commented as he made his way past the last of the vehicles and decided they had seen everything that needed to be seen on this street.

John pulled into his driveway after 11 p.m. that night to a darkened home. His parents must have called it a night shortly before. John shook his head, talking to himself.

"Man, I hope that doesn't become me someday."

However, in the back of his mind he realized that one day life will be different for him and not the same as it is now.

"If now is the time to enjoy life, why is it so difficult to have much fun?" John asked himself, realizing his life would change dramatically in only a few short months. He partially looked forward to it, while he also wondered if he would still have nights at a movie with friends. He hoped he'd still be dating Amber next year, but only time could answer that question. For now, he figured he'd better enjoy the Super Bowl party the next day and enjoy himself. At least he knew he'd have a better Sunday than some of his basketball teammates.

The next morning, John poured milk into his cereal as his parents moved about the kitchen getting breakfasts ready before church.

"So how did your outing go last night?" John's mom asked him, pouring some coffee.

"Good, it didn't go quite as expected, however."

"How's that?" John's dad asked while sitting at the kitchen table.

"Well, there was a party," John said. "And it looked like some of my basketball teammates were there."

"Really, don't they know they could get in trouble," Betty asked.

"Apparently they didn't, but now they know," John explained. "I saw the party, because I passed by it on the way to pick up Amber last night. We drove by shortly before I came home last night and saw the cops were there."

"How many people were there?" Rick asked casually.

"Plenty. Lots of cars everywhere, including Braden's. Like I told my friends, Monday will be interesting to say the least. I just hope Coach Thompson doesn't take it out on me because of the knuckleheads he chooses to start each game."

"So what are your plans for today," Betty asked John.

"I wanted to work out at the YMCA early this afternoon and then of course have Amber and Courtney over."

"Why don't you invite that nice freshman boy, Steve, over," Betty encouraged. "Does he have any freshmen friends he could bring over as well?"

"Some kid named Henry I guess. I guess I can ask Steve today. I'm not sure he's a Super Bowl party kind of guy. Since he doesn't say much, I'm not sure there will be a lot for him to do."

"Oh, I'm sure there will be something," Betty prodded John. "You have a few games in the basement you could bring up."

"I'm not sure 'Chutes and Ladders' is the kind of game high-schoolers play, but we'll see."

"Don't you have that pop-o-shot game that's collecting dust down there?" Rick said between bites of scrambled eggs.

"Yeah, I guess."

That afternoon, John stopped by Amber's house for lunch with her family and Courtney, as they shared the latest news on the previous night's activities.

"I asked one of the girls who was at the party who was there, and they said the entire boys' basketball starting lineup," Courtney stated.

"Yeah, that doesn't surprise me," John replied.

"Is coach going to do anything about it?" Amber asked.

"Who knows? Maybe a slap on the wrist, but I don't think they'll get hit too hard. Coach wants to win, and I'm sure he believes he can't win without them."

"So what time do you want us there tonight?" Courtney asked.

"Uh, how about 5? Does that work?"

"Sure," Amber said, with Courtney echoing the same sentiments.

"That reminds me, my mom wanted me to invite Steve and his friend Henry. Not sure if this'll be their thing or not, but I can ask. The dude lost his grandfather recently, so it's the least I can do."

"Sure," Amber said.

John called Steve from Amber's house see if he was interested in the get-together.

"Hey Steve, how are you?"

"Good," Steve responded quietly.

"So how would you like to come over my house to watch the Super Bowl tonight? You can invite Henry."

"Umm, I don't like football."

"That's fine, Courtney and Amber are coming over, and they're not huge football fans, either."

"I don't know."

"Well, you have my number. If you change your mind and want to come over, just give me a call."

"OK, thanks."

"You doing OK, Steve?"

"Yeah."

John listened carefully. He still could not read Steve, whether this was the best day of his life or the worst. After trying to befriend him, he realized he probably did not have too many days that are a lot of fun. John wondered whether it was simply a social issue or whether he just hated his life. John couldn't get enough out of him to reach a conclusion.

"Looks like it will just be the three of us for tonight, unless you count my parents, who will party pretty hard," John said.

"Really, your parents party hard?" Courtney asked skeptically.

"Oh yeah, I once saw my dad put down his newspaper and hit the coffee pretty hard. It was wild."

"Parents are supposed to be boring," Amber said. "Children supposedly suck the lives out of them."

"What are my parents' excuses, then?" John asked. "I'm an only child."

"Were you an extraordinarily difficult child?" Courtney asked. "You tortured your parents so much, they decided to only have one!"

"Is it true only children are weird?" Amber asked with a laugh.

"No!" John responded defensively. "I'm living proof that only children can turn out perfectly normal."

Courtney looked at him. "Problem is, you're neither perfect, nor normal."

"Maybe you're just a poor judge of character." John joked. "Didn't you tell me that that Matt the bully was a good guy?"

"I never said that!"

"Well, before I de-invite you, I better go. See you tonight?"

With that, John drove home. He looked forward to working out that afternoon, in preparation for whatever the week of basketball may hold. Once at the YMCA, he didn't recognize anyone from his school but saw plenty of high schoolers who attended one of the other schools in town. He fired up shot after shot, trying to feel good about his game and dribbled up and down the court, working on ball handling. After a couple hours, John felt confident he was ready for Monday's practice. He figured it wasn't necessary to be ready for Tuesday's home game considering the coach kept him on the bench following his banishment.

After John arrived home from his workout, his parents reminded him he needed to pick up pizzas shortly before his guests arrived.

"Yeah," John said casually, heading to the bathroom to shower.

"So John," his mother began as he passed.

"Oh boy," John thought to himself. "That's never what I want to hear."

"I wanted to talk to you about Amber. You're dating her, right?"

"Something like that."

"Is she nice?"

"No, she's quite mean, which is why I like her so much. I find the fact that she tortures innocent souls incredibly attractive."

"OK, OK. So maybe that was a dumb question. Why didn't you say anything?"

"Well, for starters I didn't really want to have a conversation like this, and second, there's really not much to say."

"She seems very nice from the times we said hello at church, it seems like you made a good selection."

"Well, I'm glad she meets your expectations."

John walked down the hall. He suddenly regretted having his friends over to his parents' place.

John made it back home with dinner before the doorbell

rang announcing the arrival of his guests.

"Hey John," Courtney said excitedly as she entered the door with Amber.

"Hi, come on in."

"This is so cool being able to see your house!"

"Yeah, well I built it with my own two hands after I made my fortune in the oil business."

"Was the first million the hardest to get?" Amber asked.

"Yes, but I'd give it all away for just a little bit more."

"So, can we have a tour?" Courtney asked.

"Sure, which wing of the castle would you like to see first?"

"The West Chamber, please," Courtney responded.

As John led them down the hall, he pointed toward his bedroom.

"That's where the mastermind does his work," John joked.

Courtney boldly walked in, with Amber tailing her.

"Nice," Amber said. "Did you clean up just for us?"

"Actually not," John answered. "I'm not a huge slob."

"That's surprising, I hear most guys are," Courtney added.

"Well, that's because you keep hanging with that Matt guy," John joked. "He has voodoo dolls and torture equipment throughout his room."

"Of course," Courtney added. "What do you think Amber, you have a clean guy?"

Amber blushed. "Yeah, this is nice."

Courtney smiled at Amber, hoping to embarrass both of them further. "You have him half trained before you even start."

"What am I, a pet or something?"

John enjoyed pizza and football with his friends that evening, thinking to himself this was as good as it gets this year considering the problems he encountered. No bullies, angry coaches, or arrogant teammates.

"So John, how did you get into basketball?" Amber asked, taking John from his thoughts.

"I started young, playing club basketball in elementary school with Braden," John explained. "He talked me into joining him in first grade, and we played every year since then. I'd always pass him the ball in the post in games, because I knew what he did well. We played at the court at his house or the park year-round and knew what we did best. It was fun."

"Until this year?" Courtney asked.

"Yeah."

"It must be weird to lose your best friend after all these years," Amber stated.

"Yep, gone just like that. He probably thought he 'outgrew' the friendship because the big boys on the team wanted to hang out with him, but no one cares about a backup. Just the way it is."

After an evening of fun, John snapped back to reality the following morning as the warning bell rang before first-hour class. He walked into the classroom just as Braden entered the door.

"Have a good time at the party the other night?" John asked with a grin.

Chapter 8

For once, Braden did not offer a response to John's remark. He just looked at him as he passed and plopped into a seat. None of the other basketball players attended the class, so John could not hear the conversations he figured may happen in the aftermath. Shortly into the hour, the principal peeked into the classroom.

"Excuse me. Sorry to interrupt, but can I talk with Braden for a bit?" The principal politely asked, as the teacher nodded. Braden collected his items and headed for the door with no expression on his face. John knew a mature person shouldn't feel happiness about seeing someone in this kind of mess, but he knew his teammates should pay for their bad decisions over the weekend. He also had a difficult time feeling sorry for them after all the punishment they put him through.

Between classes, John walked alongside Amber on their way to the next class.

"So the principal pulled Braden from class," John said with a slight grin.

"Yeah, a couple of your teammates and several girls all left with one of the principals, too," Amber said excitedly.

"How many basketball players were in your class?"

"I think just the two of them. Rashad Alexander and DaVonte Keys."

"That's three of the five starters right there."

As they walked to class, John saw Coach Thompson walk past him with a frustrated and determined look on his face.

He did not greet John and just stormed past students in the hall.

"Looks like he's gonna have a great day," John remarked with a smirk on his face.

"You don't feel bad for him?" Amber asked. "He did let you back on the team."

"True, but he's not exactly held the starters accountable. It just doesn't seem like he holds everyone to the same standards. If Braden had pushed me, there's no way he'd be off the team or even be kicked out of practice. It'll be fun to see what he does with this. He may be forced to punish the guys he never wants to blame for anything."

"What could he have done to prevent this?"

"How about promoting some team unity for starters? Notice how the whole team wasn't there at the party? The starters didn't want the backups there. They like the idea of an exclusive party," John responded.

At lunch that day, John sat with Courtney and Amber. As they ate, Steve walked tentatively over to their table and looked at John.

"So what's going on?" Steve said quietly.

"What do you mean?" John sat, while sticking a potato chip in his mouth.

"My whole class was talking about how some students got in trouble over the weekend."

"That's true, but I'm not exactly sure who did what. I'm sure I'll find out something tonight at practice. There was a big party Saturday night, and a lot of people were there."

"Oh, OK."

With that, Steve walked away.

"Interesting guy," Courtney said.

"Yeah," John said, watching him walk away. "Haven't figured him out yet."

"So what if almost everyone on your team was at the party and got in trouble?" Courtney asked John.

"I'm guessing only a few guys were there, and it's unlikely they will cancel the season or forfeit games. That's not going to happen when we're doing so well. Maybe coach will find a way to blame me for everything and let the starters continue to run wild."

A few hours later, John entered the locker room, wondering what might happen next. A few of the starters sat and talked quietly in one corner of the room. They looked up as John walked by.

DaVonte Keys peered at John from his seat. "Shouldn't you be sweeping the floor for us right now?"

"Shouldn't you be cleaning up the alcohol you spilled Saturday night?"

The guys just looked at each other.

John laughed. "I heard you were so drunk, DaVonte, that you thought Damon's washing machine was a space shuttle!"

"What if I bust you up right now, John?"

"Go for it, you can get yourself in even more trouble. We'll see who likes riding the pines now."

Two of DaVonte's teammates restrained him as he lunged toward John.

"He's not worth it," Joe Anthony said, trying to calm him.

"Looking for someone to blame other than yourself?" John asked DaVonte. "Look in the mirror."

John felt emboldened by the fact his teammates had to restrain themselves to not make their coach even angrier at them.

The team gathered at mid-court after shooting around for a few minutes as coach summoned everyone together.

"Have a seat, gentlemen, we have a lot to talk about."

John found a seat on the hard floor, a safe distance from the most volatile teammates.

"I have to say, I am greatly disappointed in some of you. We are trying to have a special season here, one that we have been building to for several years. This is supposed to be our year. We have the talent to make a playoff run this year, so that's what makes this so difficult. I've been informed all five guys in our starting lineup attended a party and were cited for underage drinking this weekend."

John sat still as the gym became dead quiet.

"Some of you guys who were at the party chose self over team," Coach Thompson said, pausing to look his team in the eye. "You made a decision that may cost us some of our season. Due to your behavior, those of you who participated in this party will miss the last few games of the regular season while the rest of you will have to pick it up."

Teammates looked at each other, realizing the season just changed.

"I've decided to call up two of our sophomores who are junior varsity players to give us a couple more options off the bench. We will have 10 guys available, then, for the remaining games. All five of our starters chose to party away the rest of the regular season, so you will be sitting on the bench in warm-up suits and cheering on your teammates, who chose to stay out of trouble. So here's how practice will work. The remaining eight guys who are eligible to play will assume the first and second team today, while those suspended will help get them ready for tomorrow's game. Got it?"

DaVonte Keys broke the silence. "The rest of the regular season? Come on coach, that's crazy. It was just one party."

John knew Coach Thompson's face would turn red in an instant, and he was not wrong about that.

"Hey, you're lucky to be playing at all," Coach Thompson screamed. "If you had cared about the team and winning, you wouldn't have been engaging in illegal behavior. And if you guys want to play for this team again, I'd suggest you keep your mouths shut, heads down and work hard these next couple of weeks if you'd like to see the court come regionals."

No one else challenged their angry coach, who blew his whistle to begin practice. After going through extra conditioning sessions, John worked with the newly-minted second team. He introduced himself to the two sophomore recruits, forward Rob Dixon and guard DeShaun Porter. The Leopards hosted last-place Lincoln High the following night, which John knew was a good chance for his squad to have a good showing. The new first unit scrimmaged the suspended group of five to get ready for the game. John sat on the side with the two sophomores discussing the new situation.

"So tomorrow, we have a good chance to get off to a good start without our normal team," John explained to Rob and DeShaun. "It's a home game against the worst team in our conference, so we have to beat them, otherwise coach might find a new team. Or he could just lift the suspensions and say we need to win games."

John worked with Juan Hernandez, Erick Samuels and the two sophomores as they ran the offense. Juan ran the show, passing the ball inside whenever he could to Erick and Rob. John took advantage of his opportunities against the zone defense, hitting a couple threes and passing to open teammates. As practice concluded, John felt good about the session and hoped Coach Thompson noticed his efforts. As the players headed to the locker room, Coach Thompson pulled John aside.

"John, make sure you're ready to go tomorrow night."

"OK, I will."

"You'll be one of the guys coming off the bench, so be ready."

John nodded and followed his teammates.

At the locker room, John caught up with his new teammates.

"So Rob and DeShaun, welcome to the team."

"Thanks, man," DeShaun said, shaking John's hand, as Rob stuck his hand out as well.

"You guys ready to go tomorrow?"

"I guess," Rob added. "This is kind of crazy going from JV to varsity, especially when some upper classmen didn't make the team in November."

"I hear you," John replied. "Don't worry about that, just play your game when you get in. You don't have to be the stars like on JV. You just need to play solid ball and not mess anything up. Don't turn the ball over."

"I'll keep that in mind," DeShaun stated. "So what's the team like? I've never talked to any of these guys before."

John chuckled. "That may not change even though you're now on the team."

"What do you mean?" Rob asked.

"Kind of a clicky bunch. You know, starters talk to starters, benchwarmers to benchwarmers. And no one talks to me, because I was briefly kicked off the team for fighting one of the starters at the end of practice."

"Wow, really?" Rob asked, surprised.

"Really. The backups can be nice enough guys. At least they were until I came back on the team. No one gets along too well, though. Why do you think only the starting five got busted at the party? They weren't gonna hang out with scrubs and de-invited them."

The two just nodded, as John continued. "You'll have a better chance of getting along with some of the backups, who will now be playing. I have to go, so I'll see you guys later. Again, welcome to the team, and I look forward to playing alongside you tomorrow."

"Yeah, thanks for the info, man," DeShaun stated.

As John headed out of the locker room, he saw the starters mingling among themselves, complaining about the punishment. Rashad Alexander spotted John leaving.

"John, dude, you're gonna sink our season, huh? You blow it tomorrow and you're getting blamed."

"Oh, jeez, I don't want to lose your respect," John replied mockingly. "You're the one who chose to drink like a camel. But go ahead, keep blaming other people. See where that gets you in life."

"As always, shut up, John," Braden remarked.

"What's the matter, big man, you screw up and you don't want anybody mad at you? As Mr. Keys here always says, 'Have fun on the bench.'"

"We'll be back come playoff time," DaVonte added, getting in on the conversation.

"Hope you're not rusty, because the season will be over before you can down another beer."

That evening, Amber stopped by John's house to study.

"So you ready to go tomorrow night?" Amber asked, flipping through her textbook as they studied at the kitchen table.

"We'll see, I may not even get in the game. They could use just two backups or they could pass me up to give the two JV guys time. Coach did ask me to be ready, but he could change his mind by tomorrow. I'm not holding my breath, but I'll be ready. If the other guys stink it up, he may have to play me and see what happens."

"Why wouldn't he play you?"

"The same weird reasons he hasn't put me in a single game since I rejoined the team. I don't know. He just made an example out of me. It will be interesting to see which side of coach wins out, the disciplinarian or the guy who wants to win at all costs. If we start to lose, maybe he'll reinstate the starters just so we can get a higher seed in the regionals. We'll see what kind of moral fiber he has."

"My first choir concert is in March, you're coming right?"

"Yeah, of course. That's a ways off, isn't it?"

"I just wanted to make sure."

"You've come out to a lot of my games, so the least I can do is go to your concerts since they don't have that many of them."

"Thanks. I'm looking forward to seeing you sitting somewhere other than on the bench."

"Thanks, I guess. I'd like to have a change in scenery too."

Despite John's skepticism with the idea he might actually check into a game, he couldn't help but feel excited about the game and wished classes went quickly that day instead of the long hours he endured.

As John made a snack before heading to the game, his parents passed him in the kitchen.

"You coming out to the game tonight?" John asked, looking up from his plate.

"We have plans tonight, as we do on other Tuesday nights," John's mother reminded him.

"Of course."

"John, we can't put our lives aside just to watch a meaningless game where you won't even play. We're not that interested in basketball and have other obligations."

John didn't respond, unwilling to push the issue. His friends' attendance was enough.

As John warmed up a couple hours later, he looked over at the Lincoln High players warming up and realized they had to win tonight to avoid embarrassment and a further rift between teammates. He knew the starters will give the backups a bad time if they mess up and cost them a game, even though they should only blame themselves for this situation.

As John took his seat just a couple of players away from where Coach Thompson sat, he looked in the stands to see if he recognized anyone. John spotted Amber and Courtney perched near the top of the bleachers and the Harmons sitting near mid-court. He wondered if any of the guys playing tonight would talk to him now that they are playing together in an actual game. Juan Hernandez and Erick Samuel sat to his left, while the two new teammates sat to his right.

John turned to Juan and Erick as the PA announcer readied to announce the starting lineup.

"And now, announcing the drinking All-Stars," John stated, trying to imitate a deep-voiced announcer. "At point guard, he can climb on a wagon as fast as he can fall off it, Rashad Alexander."

Juan and Erick chuckled, but tried not to encourage John.

"At forward, he can hold a basketball better than he can hold his liquor, DaVonte Keys. And at forward, he carries a 12-pack with him to school for lunch each day, Joe Anthony."

"You're really enjoying this, aren't you?" Erick stated.

"After the way they've treated me, I can revel just a little bit, can't I? This is the only way we're getting in a game, so you better not complain."

"What if we stink it up?" Erick asked.

"Don't talk like that, we'll play well," John said confidently.

John did not move any closer to the coach as his two teammates went into the game a few minutes into the first quarter with North leading 10-7. Darnell Jackson and Sam Stevens took a seat next to John, using their jerseys to wipe sweat from their foreheads. John refrained from saying anything to them, fearing they may ignore him once again. At the end of the first quarter, North held a 14-13 lead. John joined the huddle as the buzzer sounded, listening to Coach Thompson's advice. He felt weird standing in the huddle when normally he stood behind everyone and pretended to listen alongside the other backups. He knew the message was for those who actually took the court and not him.

Midway through the second quarter, Coach Thompson tapped John on the shoulder.

"Go in for Dominique."

"Yep," John said, taking off his warm-up shirt and jogging to the scorer's table.

He looked up at the scoreboard, which showed North in the lead, 20-19. John knew if they did not play better, Coach Thompson would put on a verbal show for his captive halftime audience. John wondered whether Darnell would pass him the ball or try to force passes into double teams. He looked up at the crowd as he made his way across the floor for his first meaningful action of the year. John jogged down the court as Darnell handled the ball, ready to run the offense. He never touched the ball the first two possessions, as his teammates found shots in the post.

John's frustration began to build when his teammates turned the ball over a couple times and missed makeable shots. Lincoln took a 25-22 lead with a couple minutes to go before halftime. As Darnell committed another turnover by throwing a pass that bounced off a teammate's foot, John walked over to him.

"Let's go, we have to get this turned around, or we'll never get in another game again. We're embarrassing ourselves."

"Worry about yourself."

"Why? Apparently worrying about yourself is all you're doing right now. How about a little team play? It's OK to not force the ball into the post."

Darnell walked away as Lincoln inbounded the ball. As the opponent swung the ball from one side of the arc to the other, Terrance White got a hand on the ball, which bounced toward John. He grabbed it and dribbled down court, spotting Dan Zimmerman open to his right. John fired a pass to his teammate, who returned the ball as soon as John's defender ran to cover Dan. John reeled in the pass just behind the three-point arc and without hesitation put up the shot, which swished through the net. A few cheers emerged from quiet crowd, as the game now stood at a 25-25 tie. John took a deep breath and felt the joy of playing the game of basketball for the first time in what seemed like forever. The two teams failed to score the rest of the half, leaving the score tied at 25.

The Leopards jogged to the locker room to half-hearted fan applause, which John expected from the crowd that counted on an easy victory over Lincoln. Coach Thompson exuded his usual halftime personality, hollering at assorted players for their lack of execution. The coach excluded John from his wrath, which he figured may be due to the fact he ignored him so long that it may be difficult to start a new trend so late in the season. John wondered how much he would play in the second half but figured he may get a few minutes. He looked over at Coach Thompson, who finished his fiery tirade.

"We should be beating these guys by 20 points!" Coach Thompson bellowed. "I don't care who's in the game, we need to get it done. I expect everyone in the game to pick up their efforts. We shouldn't be missing short jumpers and layups. It's inexcusable. Go out there and show that you know how to play basketball. If not, I'll find someone who can, even if I have to pull students from the stands."

As players jogged back to the court, John smiled and looked over at Erick Samuels.

"Now that's confidence in your team right there," John said.

"You better start making your shots, or coach will pull the most unathletic popcorn-eating all-star out of the stands he can find and replace you."

Erick just shook his head, trying not to laugh.

"Dude, does he always give speeches like that?" DeShaun Porter asked John.

"Pretty much every game," John replied. "Don't worry, the yelling starts to lose its affect after a while. I barely hear him anymore, especially since the rants never concern me. He only yells at the important people."

As expected, John sat on the bench to start the third quarter, with the new starting group back in. Both teams turned the ball over frequently and missed shots, giving the fans an ugly exhibition. The Leopards trailed 35-30 halfway through the third quarter when Coach Thompson called all five reserves over to the scorer's table and told them in a few words to play better than those currently running the show.

John looked over at the two sophomores, who displayed wide eyes as they realized their first varsity action approached. He leaned over to Rob and DeShaun.

"Just relax. Don't try to do too much. Take care of the ball with good passes and play hard on defense. Got it?"

They both nodded.

"These aren't all-stars on Lincoln," John continued. "You guys can play with them. Stick to your game."

Once in the contest, Juan Hernandez dribbled the ball down the court and then tried to zip John a pass. A Lincoln guard tipped the pass, while his teammates scooped it up and took the ball toward the basket for an easy layup.

"Come on!" Coach Thompson yelled from the sideline.

On the next possession Juan got the ball to John without incident and then dumped the ball off to Rob in the post, who tentatively gave the ball back to John. He used a ball fake to get his defender off of him and then took a couple of dribbles to his left before sinking another three to close the gap to 37-33. By the end of the quarter, Lincoln held a 40-37 advantage.

John used his jersey to wipe sweat off his forehead as he huddled with his teammates before the start of the fourth quarter. He had not played this long of a stretch since his junior varsity days. Coach Thompson looked like he had been on the court judging the amount of sweat on his face.

"We're going to make some changes right now," coach explained. "John, I want you running point with all of the starters back in the game except Darnell. You'll go in for John at point in a bit. I want the turnovers to stop now, OK? We've got to play better defense and make some shots, but we can't do that when we're turning the ball over. Gentlemen, we have to win this game. I don't want to lose on our home court to a last-place team, so we've got to find a way to get it done!"

John looked over at the starters, who wore warm-up suits and sat at the end of the bench, standing behind the group huddled around coach. They chatted quietly, hoping coach would not notice their lack of attention.

"If we were in, we'd be up 20 right now," junior forward Joe Alexander said, shaking his head.

"These guys are scrubs," Rashad Alexander responded. "They don't deserve to be playing. We should be out there winning the game instead of us having to sit here and watch these chumps get whooped by a sorry team like Lincoln."

"Coach can have these losers," DaVonte Keys added. "When we get back, we'll show who the real players on this team are."

At that moment, Darnell Jackson looked over at DaVonte.

"Seriously, man? We're in the middle of a game and you're dissing us?"

"Maybe if you knew how to play ball we wouldn't be

talking. You know you're only out there for a few games and then it's us again."

"What are you talking about?" Darnell fired back. "I'm one of the first guys coming in to give you guys a break every game. I ain't no scrub."

"But you be playing like one right now!" Teyshaun White said, to the howl of his teammates' laughter.

John ran back on the court to free himself of the escalating situation near the bench. His teammates followed suit, but he saw Coach Thompson walk over to the argument. A couple of the starters kept talking at Darnell, who suddenly lost his temper and pushed DaVonte in the chest as coach stepped between them. John didn't hear what DaVonte said, but he did hear Coach Thompson.

"Get on the end of the bench!" Coach screamed. "Haven't you guys got in enough trouble? And Darnell, you're not going back in. Have a seat at the end of the bench."

"Well, there goes another player," John remarked to Sam Stevens. "You realize about half the team's gotten in trouble? What a season."

"Yeah, well, you got in trouble, not me," Sam responded coolly.

"But you'll probably still talk to Darnell, right? Even though he just went after a teammate. Otherwise, you can keep kissing the starters' butts like everyone else."

Sam just glared at John, but he kept talking.

"You better pick up your game right now, Sam, otherwise we're done tonight."

"Worry about yourself."

John walked over to the other three players on the court and asked them to huddle.

"Guys, get in here, I gotta say something," John instructed. "Look, the starters are talking smack about us not being able to play. I think we can get the job done if we just concentrate and get control of our nerves. It's just basketball. Let's do what we do against the starters in practice and get after it. We can beat these guys, just like everybody else does. This is our one chance to show we can play. Let's get out there and get after it!"

The four other players nodded in agreement and found their places on the court. John dribbled the ball up court with confidence, realizing he will likely be on the court longer due to Darnell's sudden suspension. The Leopards began clawing their way back, as the forwards began to hit a couple shots inside and Dominique Carter and Terrance White began hitting a couple of jumpers. On defense, John gave his best effort, hoping everyone else would follow his lead. He knocked a ball loose and fired off a pass to Dominique before he landed on the floor. Dominique dribbled toward the hoop and passed the ball to Terrance, who raced to the rim for a layup. The crowd came alive, trying to will the team to a comeback victory. John could not get a couple of jumpers to fall late in the game, but the Leopards remained in the game. With 57 seconds remaining, the score stood tied at 52.

As the teams huddled, John tried to catch his breath. Juan came into the game for him in the middle of the quarter for a short break, but he had played most of the second half. He realized the irony of the fact he played so little all season and now played so many minutes he was exhausted. John knew he had to muster enough energy for this last minute. Lincoln had the ball and planned to run the clock. The team passed the ball back and forth near mid-court, keeping the ball from North and then began to run their offense with under 30 seconds left. A forward popped open under the basket with 10 seconds left, and the point guard found him. The opponent put the ball in the basket, making the score 54-52 with 10 seconds remaining. North called their final timeout to discuss their plan.

"Look, they're going to press, so we need to break it and still get a good look," Coach Thompson explained.

John felt weird sitting on the bench facing his coach. He typically looked into the huddle from the outside the last couple of years and felt awkward being one of the guys the coach actually talked with during breaks. Coach Thompson set up a play to get Dominique the ball on the wing, with an option to toss the ball inside to Dan Zimmerman.

As the players walked back onto the court, John looked over at Sam.

"I'm just going to shoot a half-courter, OK?"

"How can you joke at a time like this?" Sam responded.

"You gotta put aside your nerves right now, man."

Sam inbounded the ball to John, who immediately drew two defenders. John took one dribble to his left and passed to Terrance who dribbled up court and then passed the ball over midcourt to Dominique. The defenders immediately swarmed and then trapped him above the three-point line. Dominique got off a bounce pass back to Terrance to the top of the key. John saw the clock ticking down and then realized Terrance would have to make a quick decision. When a defender ran to him a few feet above the three-point arc, Terrance looked to his left at John and tossed him the ball, unwilling to try a long three. John caught the ball a few feet behind the arc, took one dribble and confidently shot the three-pointer.

The buzzer sounded as the ball swished through the net, giving the Leopards the 55-54 win. John turned to the crowd and pumped his fist. For the first time since the beginning of the season, his teammates treated him as one of their own, surrounding him in a congratulatory hug. The crowd roared, shocked by the Leopards' ability to avoid an upset.

"We did it!" John exclaimed, as one of his teammates lifted him off the ground.

John looked over at Sam. "Was this better than a half-courter?"

Sam shook his head, "You're one cool cat, man. I didn't think we could pull this one out."

John looked over the gym and saw the suspended starting group showing little enthusiasm. They milled around near the bench and then made their way to the locker room.

"That's typical," John said to the teammates next to him. "They want us to cheer for them, but they sure as heck can't cheer anyone else on."

John's teammates followed his gaze toward the starting five exiting the gym. A familiar voice then caught John's attention.

"Hey John, congratulations!" Don Harmon said, standing alongside his wife, Julie.

"Thanks."

"You played a heck of a game and hit the game winner, you can't do any better than that!"

"My teammates had more to do with it than I did," John said, as several of his teammates still milled around him. "We just hung in there and kept after it."

"Well great job," Don said enthusiastically. "We'll see you tomorrow, right?"

"Yeah, thanks for coming out to the game."

As the couple walked away, Amber and Courtney strolled up to John.

"Nice going!" Amber said.

"Yeah, you played great!" Courtney added.

"Thanks, it was a lot of fun and everyone on our team played well.

"Say, what was up with the fight on your bench?" Courtney asked.

"I don't know. Some of the starters being jerks again. They gave Darnell a bad time because we weren't beating Lincoln and they started to mock him. They're just mad because they're suspended. Anyway, Coach Thompson suspended Darnell for the rest of the game, so that makes seven of us he's benched this season."

"Maybe you coach isn't doing something right if everyone's getting suspended," Amber said.

"Oh, no," John said sarcastically. "It couldn't possibly be his fault."

"So did coach know you were going to take the last shot?" Courtney ask.

"No, of course not. He drew the play up for another player, but it was just the way it worked out. I better get going, but I'll see you both tomorrow, right?"

"Of course. Again, great job, John," Amber said.

John headed to the locker room to get changed. As he entered the room, he saw a couple of his teammates attempting to console a disgruntled Darnell Jackson.

"Dude, let it go," Dominique Carter told him. "You don't want to fight those guys, it'll be bad for everyone."

"I played every game with them and this is how they do me? They get me in trouble just because we weren't playing as well as them? That's garbage, man."

As John finished dressing, he followed Darnell out of the locker room, curious about what might happen next.

John opened the locker room door to hear the sounds of disagreement.

"I can't believe you went at me, Darnell," DaVonte said to Darnell, who wore a scowl on his face.

"If I had known one push would get me out of the game, I'd have gotten my money's worth and punched you out, man," Darnell responded.

"I'd love to see you try," DaVonte taunted. "You'd be on the floor in about two seconds."

John pulled out his phone and began taking a video of what might go down.

"You guys are just a bunch of scrubs," DaVonte continued. "You needed a lucky shot from cheap-shot John over here just to beat a worthless team like Lincoln. We'd have put'em away in the first quarter. You guys have no business being on the court. We're winners and you guys are nothing.'"

John kept the phone in position where it didn't look like he was recording. He was unconcerned about recording the footage, as long as he got the audio of these comments. This was good stuff.

"Is that what you think of me?" Darnell asked. "I played alongside you all season. I'm just as good a point guard as Rashad and you know it. I play a lot every game, and you treat me like some backup like John, here?"

"Keep it up, Darnell," John said, "You're not making too many friends here."

"For once John's right," DaVonte stated. "You're gonna get a beating real soon."

With that, Darnell launched himself at DaVonte, pushing him up against the wall while his teammates pulled him off. John held up his phone at this point from a few feet away, not caring if anyone saw. Darnell gave up at this point and stormed off silently. John hit the stop button on his phone and slipped it in his pocket.

"You guys are great teammates," John said, walking away.

"Yeah, well you're headed back to the bench soon, where you belong," DaVonte shouted as John kept walking. As he rounded the corner, he saw Darnell punch a locker.

"Be careful with your hand, man," John warned. "You may need it the next game."

"Leave me alone," Darnell snapped.

"Now you know how it feels, huh Darnell? How do you think I felt about how you acted toward me and how everyone treated me just because of one mistake? I was ticked off about the way the starters treated me and I acted pretty much just like you did there."

Darnell just stared at him.

"Let it go and ignore those guys. They'll get theirs. Just worry about playing the game and everything will work out."

Darnell continued his silence.

"Look, I don't dislike anyone, including you, even though you and everyone else treated me like garbage. You're now getting what I got from some of the guys, which is why I lost it. Now you have a choice to make."

"What choice?"

"I got it all on my phone. Come in with me to chat with coach. Otherwise you'll just get in the same trouble trying to fight an unwinnable battle against those guys."

"Wait, you want me to visit coach while he looks at a video where I'm fighting someone again? He just suspended me for doing that in a game!"

"True, but how much more trouble can you get in? Besides, it'll make them look a lot worse than you, especially if the team sees it. They're ripping their teammates. You're just standing up for yourself."

"Maybe."

"Come on, now's the time to do this, what do you say?"

Chapter 9

Darnell looked intently at John, weighing the pros and cons of whether to visit Coach Thompson to show him the video.

"OK, let's do it."

"Good to hear," John said. "Coach may realize he made a mistake suspending you, and it may keep him from suspending you for the next game because of what happened on the bench."

"Why are you even talking to me? I gave you crap for trying to take out Braden."

"Yeah, well, so did everyone else, although you did give me more grief than some. You can be a pretty mean guy, what's with that?"

Darnell did not say anything, not sure how to respond.

"Look man, you didn't like your teammates ragging on you. They did what you had been doing to me."

"Yeah, OK."

"Golden Rule, man. And now you're in the same situation I was in. You either have to fight back, which as I am finding out is impossible, or just take it. They already don't like us, why not let coach do something about it? And if he doesn't, we'll have to weigh our options then. It'll be pretty tough for him to not do anything about this."

"So when do you want to do this?"

"Tomorrow morning before school. Get it out of the way. That work?"

"Yep, I'll meet you at his office."

"See you then."

John's parents greeted him as he walked into his house a few minutes later, feeling exhausted but happy despite the recent incident.

"How'd the game go?" his mother asked half-heartedly.

"Good," John said.

"Did you play?" his father asked, taking his eyes off a television program.

"Yeah, hit the game-winning shot."

"Really? That's something."

"I wish I had parents who cared," John thought to himself as walked into his room and tossed his gym bag on his bed. "Always too busy to attend such a trivial event."

John watched the video on his phone to make sure he recorded everything he wanted. He knew now was the time to act if he wanted the bullying to stop. Now that he was not the only victim made it a stronger case.

The next morning John saw Darnell standing outside coach's office.

"You got the video?"

"Yes sir, I watched it last night to make sure I got everything. And it's all there."

"Good, let's do this."

John knocked on the wooden door and heard coach summon them a moment later.

"Come on in," Coach Thompson said while looking at a pile of papers at his desk. "What can I do for you John and Darnell?"

Darnell looked at John, who took the lead. "I hate to bother you, but we thought you should see a video I have. As I may have mentioned, your starting five have been jerks this year, and now they're coming after Darnell."

Coach Thompson looked at them through the bottom of his

reading glasses.

"And Darnell wants me to listen after I had to bench him last night?"

Darnell finally spoke. "Like he said. Now they're coming after me and dividing the team."

Coach Thompson nodded his head. "So when did all this start?"

"During yesterday's game," Darnell responded.

Coach Thompson looked at John.

"Most of the season for me," John said. "Especially after I came back to the team. I didn't want to say anything at first because I just wanted to try to get along, but it's been relentless, and nothing I can do will get them to stop. They're doing to Darnell and others what they've been doing to me for a while. After enough of this stuff, you just snap. I shouldn't have done what I did, and Darnell shouldn't have done what he did, but this is tough. The starting five are calling everyone scrubs."

"So what do you want to show me?"

"This," John said, hitting play on his phone.

Coach Thompson watched the video, not saying anything. As the video finished, John saw Coach Thompson turning red.

"I'll take care of it."

John and Darnell sat silently, waiting for Coach Thompson to say something more.

"Thanks for stopping by, some of the guys will have an interesting practice tonight."

As the two seniors walked out of their coach's office, they looked at each other, not sure what to make of the meeting.

"Well, things can't get any worse," John said with a smirk. "Maybe this will help.

"Or some our teammates will kill us, at which point things could get worse," Darnell responded. "I have to say, though, dude, that was a smart move with the phone recording."

"Tough to get away with stuff these days with technology. Maybe I should do that every time someone does something bad to me. Help keep them honest. Well, I'll see you at practice tonight."

"Yeah, I'll see ya."

After what felt like an eternity of classes, basketball practice arrived. John got out to the gym as quickly as possible to take as many jumpers as he could hoist before the coach's whistle blew. He noticed the starting five all sat together in the locker room, not communicating with the other players. After a brief shoot around, Coach Thompson called the team together.

"Have a seat gentlemen," the coach shouted.

"We've heard this one before, haven't we?" Sam Stevens said quietly to those around him. "He realizes this floor is tough to sit on, right?"

"So what's harder, the floor or the bench, Sam?" Rashad Alexander snapped at him.

"Why ask me? You're getting some experience at both."

"Oh, burn!" Darnell fired back at Rashad.

Coach Thompson interrupted their conversation. "Listen up! It's come to my attention that even more fighting took place after the game last night, and it's my job to put an end to it. I have a few things I want to say to the suspended guys, so hear me well. If you want to ever see the court again, you're going to support those in the game, like they supported you all season. I don't care what the score is, you're going to support them. So adjust your attitudes right now if you plan to get game action again. Just remember, you won't play until the end of the regular season, so you better find a way to make do. If I find out anymore of this stuff, you'll sit in the playoffs too. You got me?"

The starting group half-heartedly nodded.

"We've got a lot of work to do in this practice if we want to be ready for Friday's game against West, so those not playing need to help those who are playing ready. I don't want more drama, so figure out how to get along with your teammates."

As the team readied for drills, Sam tried to lighten the somber mood.

"Turns out John here is a shooter and not just a fighter."

John gave him a half smile. "Where was this talk a few games ago? Would have been nice to hear something positive then."

John split time playing both shooting guard and point guard, as he figured Coach Thompson was trying to figure out where to play him and others. While at point guard, John continued to worry about the lack of team play. After Dan Zimmerman forced up a shot from the post position, John gave him a look from the top of the key.

"Dan!"

"What?"

John walked over to him. "You've got Juan open at the key. If they double on you, someone is open. This time it was Juan."

"Whatever, stop bugging me."

"But you're hurting the team. Don't you care about things, like, say, winning? Pass the ball!"

Dan appeared indifferent to John's request and kept putting up shots. John wiped sweat from his forehead as the practice neared its end. He found himself next to Rob and DeShaun as they walked off the court.

"Man, if we don't start playing team basketball, we won't win another game. Everyone's just putting up shots, mostly bad ones."

The sophomore duo nodded.

"Don't try to force stuff. There's no shot clock. Just make

good passes and eventually something will open up."

Two days later, John started the game on the bench, watching the starting group begin the game against second-place West High. The Leopards held a two-game lead over West for the conference lead, but the team knew beating them on the road was difficult. North fell behind 15-7 a few minutes into the game, as West took advantage of turnovers and took advantage of fast break points.

"We gotta stop turning the ball over, man," John said to Erick Samuels and Juan Hernandez. "When we get in there, let's take care of the basketball."

"I just want to hit some shots so maybe coach'll play me more once the starters come back," Erick said.

"Not cool, Erick," John responded. "That's not the goal, here. Don't you want to, like, see the team win?"

"I guess. Me shooting will help the team win."

John laughed. "Whatever. You may need to keep your ego in check, don't you think?"

North trailed 25-13 at the end of the first quarter, as Coach Thompson's anger increased. John stood outside the huddle, listening to his coach desperately trying to keep the train on the rails.

Coach Thompson sweated while pointing at his board. "Look, Terrance, you've got to set a good pick. You can't just let him go right by you. And Sam, why are you forcing this shot up when you have three guys on you. Pass the ball! Darnell, why are you letting the defenders trap you at mid-court?"

John looked at the scoreboard, realizing this may be a long game. Coach Thompson looked over at John and pointed. "You're in, John. Juan and Erick, you too. Darnell, Sam and Terrance, you're all getting a rest."

John enthusiastically headed for the scorer's table, with

Juan and Erick following close behind. He walked alongside Erick as they made their way onto the court.

"Remember, man, you just heard what coach said. No selfish stuff, let's get a good shot."

Juan ran point guard, while John played shooting guard. As Juan dribbled the ball up the court, John noticed the above-average height of West players, who locked down on the Leopards' offense. John had a difficult time getting an open shot and making easy passes. West pressured everything. At the next timeout, John took charge in the huddle, with Coach Thompson listening.

"We're going to have to do some backdoor cuts," John explained. "They're not sitting back on defense, so we're going to have to keep them honest."

"Good point, John," Coach Thompson stated. "We're not doing much of anything on offense and certainly not running clean plays. Everything is off, so look to go backdoor with some of these passes, as John said. Let's go, we need to get back in this thing right now!"

As the team made its way back on the court, John looked up at the stands. None of his family and friends attended this game despite the short distance between the two schools within the city limits. John tried to ignore negative thoughts about his parents' absence.

"It doesn't matter," John told himself. "I usually just sit on the bench anyway."

The game soon got away from North, as the Leopards continued to struggle. Turnovers and missed shots plagued the team, and North fell behind at the half 45-29. John made one layup on a backdoor cut, but West High forwards thwarted his other attempts to get to the basket. As the team trudged to the locker room dreading their coach's halftime fire and brimstone message, John walked alongside his

149

teammates.

"Guys, we're not out of this thing yet. We just have to play better team basketball."

"Whatever, we're getting killed," Dam Zimmerman responded.

"If you'd get me the ball more, John, maybe we would be in it," Erick snapped.

"Really? When should I have passed you the ball?"

"I've been open in the post all day."

"A second defender was sneaking up behind you every time. Didn't you see that?"

Erick became silent.

"You're right, I have been playing selfishly," John continued. "Firing off fade away threes, any shot I can get, right?"

No one said anything as they entered the locker room and sat down.

"This sucks," Dominique said, throwing a towel across the room.

"Who sucks?" Dan responded. "You took the most shots, so whose fault is this?"

"Shut up, Dan," Terrance added.

"You too, Terrance," Dan added. "You've been jacking up shots all day. You guys are taking all the shots and not hitting anything. Don't blame anyone else."

"If Darnell here would quit giving West the ball every darn possession, maybe we'd have a few more chances to make baskets," Dominique shot back.

"Now you're throwing me under the bus? I'm trying my best, man, but they're always pressing. Come up and help me once in a while. I need someone to pass the ball too."

Coach Thompson entered the room as the argument continued. "That's enough! I've never seen so much drama on a team I've coached. This needs to stop. No one's playing well, and if we keep this up, we're going to get run out of the gym. Do you guys want to be laughed at? No one else is coming in the game to relieve you. You've got to figure things out for yourself."

John heard Rashad snicker at the coach's criticism. He felt helpless, realizing those on the court got a shot to play more minutes, but played like it was the end of a lopsided game. John wondered if the team had enough talent to win more than a couple games before the postseason.

As Coach Thompson finished his speech and the team headed toward the court, those sitting the game out became vocal.

"Don't worry, guys, we'll be back to save our season," Rashad mocked. "This is what happens when scrubs get to play."

"You want me to punch your punk face in right now, Rashad?" Darnell said.

"You guys are tearing yourselves apart without our help," Rashad answered. "You should be begging us to get back on the court."

"Guess you don't care about the team, huh Rashad?" Darnell remarked.

"We're going to save the team. Coach wants to go to state, and he knows the only way to get there is to not play guys like you too much. He needs us. This is his best chance to get to state, he's not going to throw that away just to make some kind of statement about a wild party."

"Wow, you have an even bigger ego than I thought."

Rashad laughed. "I know I can get the job done, and you know you can't."

John kept walking, in a rush to get back on the court and put up some shots. He tried to ignore the negative comments the starters made. He just wanted to focus on this game. John looked around, seeing the crowd and tried to think about only the positive aspects of basketball. He enjoyed playing the game, and remembered the fact this was supposed to be fun. Maybe the Leopards will lose this game, but he could still play hard and have fun, even if his teammates made life difficult.

North continued to struggle in the second half, falling behind 61-35 by the end of the third quarter. Coach Thompson did not say much to the team in the huddle, as he resigned to the reality of defeat. After plenty of yelling to start the third quarter, John noticed his coach become quiet. He figured he must be so frustrated that he was ready to give up. Early in the fourth quarter, Rob and DeShaun checked in, replacing Dan and Dominique. The two wore wide eyes as they made their over to John.

"Hey, just relax and play ball," John advised. "Take care of the ball and wait to get good shots. It's not like anybody's expecting you to help us rally."

The Leopards trailed 70-39 a few minutes into the quarter, but with two new players in the game, North found energy. Juan played point guard, John and DeShaun filled the guard position, and Rob and Sam played forward. John hoped with Erick on the bench the team could play together and find some rhythm. North found a few fast breaks against West's starting group, as DeShaun and Rob showed speed others did not. John scored just seven points in the first three quarters but now had more opportunities with the two youngsters playing alongside him. John hit a three-pointer on a fast break, while the forwards scored points under the basket. North cut the lead to 75-55 with four minutes remaining.

After a missed West shot, Sam passed John the ball, who dribbled up the court. He noticed Rob and DeShaun striding down court, one on each side. John fired a pass to DeShaun, who kicked it back to him when the defenders closed around him. John stopped, faked a shot and then drove by his defender for a layup. The West crowd became silent, while the remaining North fans applauded politely.

West called a timeout, as their coach walked onto the court to shout at his team for their lack of effort. John chuckled to himself as he headed toward his own bench. Coach Thompson seemed a shell of his normal, boisterous self. He gave a couple of reminders but did so in a soft tone.

Erick leaned over to Dan in the huddle. "So if we just play bad enough, coach will stop yelling at us?"

"If that's the case, then I guess you did good work."

"Don't worry, Erick, you'll have plenty of chances the next game to miss more shots and turn the ball over," Dominique added.

"Like you should talk," Erick shot back. "West loved playing defense against you. How many times did they trap you at midcourt?"

"Not as many times as I'm going to hit you in a second," Dominique responded.

John tried to ignore the quarreling teammates as the coach made his final comments.

North continued to play well in the final few minutes, but could not do enough to rally, losing 79-65. John finished with 14 points, a career high.

"We nearly had them," Sam explained, attempting to console teammates.

"Are you joking or for real?" Dan Zimmerman inquired.

"We made a comeback. We just needed more time."

"Whatever, they just weren't playing that hard by the fourth quarter," Erick added.

"Dude, they still had their starters in," Juan interjected. "Maybe you're just mad that you were on the bench and unable to shoot us into a hole."

"Shut up, Juan."

John decided to join the conversation. "I told you, Erick, but you wouldn't listen. If you play team ball, you'll get your chances, but you're trying to force stuff and it just doesn't work. You're not the only one doing this, but come on, take some responsibility. Otherwise, we're going to continue to stink."

"Like you've played perfectly," Erick responded.

"I haven't, but we all need to get better. Why do you keep shooting into double teams?"

"I just haven't gotten hot yet."

"So you're going to get hot taking low percentage shots? Let me know when that happens."

"Next game."

"Can I hold you to that?"

Erick didn't respond.

Despite their coach's warning, the locker room remained a hostile environment. John hurried to get showered and changed.

"We're back on the court in just a couple weeks," Teyshaun remarked, taunting his teammates near him. "Enjoy your run of losing."

John noticed a couple of the suspended starters remained quiet, afraid their coach may overhear their comments and add further punishment.

"Hey Erick!" Rashad yelled. "Which of your air balls was your favorite? The one that missed the rim by a foot or the other one that looked like more of an alley-oop, only with no one catching it?"

Erick kept silent, not wanting to provoke the most popular and talented team members.

John walked by a fuming Erick. "Now you know how I felt

all season with some of these guys. You may want to rethink your on-court strategy or they'll give you more of this."

John left the locker room shaking his head and tiredly boarded the bus, looking forward to home. The Leopards' next game was Tuesday, one of three remaining regular season games before the playoffs. John sat by himself, trying to avoid the thoughts of the tough loss and the infighting. As the bus readied to leave, John answered his phone.

"Hi Amber, how's it going?"

"Hey John, I just finished some homework and wanted to call. How was the game?"

"It was a tough one."

"How bad?"

"We lost by 14."

"That's not so bad, considering you had all backups and they're the next best team in the conference."

"Yeah, I guess, but we didn't play well. We made a run in the fourth quarter to make it closer than it was."

"Oh."

"So, you want to do something this weekend?"

"Sure, I have to work in the morning, but I can do something later in the day."

"Awesome, what would you like to do?"

"I don't know, why don't you surprise me?"

"Uh, oh. Surprises? What if I'm not the creative type?"

"Oh, come on. You can come up with something."

"I guess. Let's see, we've already done a couple movies, a Super Bowl party and drove by someone else's party. What's left to be done in this city? I'll have to give it some thought."

"You better."

"I have to go, so I'll talk to you later."

"Good night."

John spent Saturday morning finishing homework and

trying to figure out where to take Amber that evening. He figured he better come up with something good or she might think he lacks the creative energy to stay out of a rut. After mulling this seemingly monumental decision, he decided to seek Courtney's counsel.

"So you want my help?" Courtney asked.

"Yeah, I've got nothing."

"Well, what do you want me to do about it? It's your problem."

"You know her better than I do. You've been friends with her for a long time. I'm sure you know her interests better than I do."

"Come on, you should be able to figure something out. What do you know she likes?"

"Well, I know she's in choir, so music I guess."

"Brilliant, Sherlock."

"Anything else?"

"Getting homework done on time?"

"I'm not sure that's helpful or relevant to your problem."

"OK, I'm not sure beyond that. Is there someone I can pay who can come up with somewhere cool to take her? The only problem is, I'm on a budget here."

"Yeah, maybe that person should then take her to a cool place."

"Funny. OK, I'll figure something out myself. I had no idea trying to get other people to do my work for me was so much work."

"You can do this."

"Thanks. This conversation never took place, right?"

"For a fee."

"Like I said, I'm on a budget here. I'll have to take my chances, I guess."

"Good luck."

John figured that since Amber enjoyed music, he should find a music event somewhere. However, due to his budgetary restraints, John needed a cheap concert. He checked the Internet to see what events would take place this weekend in the city.

"Bingo," John said to himself, finding a choir concert at the local college. "It's free and something I wouldn't do myself. Excellent."

Later that evening, John drove to Amber's home, where she jumped in his car a couple minutes later.

"Hey John, so where are we off to?"

"Well, dinner first and then the surprise. That way, if the surprise goes awry, you can't throw food at me."

"Yeah, well, it wouldn't be the first time you've had food thrown at you during a dinner with me. So what's up with you calling Courtney to ask her what to do?"

John laughed. "Darn that Courtney! She had one secret to keep and she couldn't do it."

"Just one secret?"

"OK, there's something I need to tell you. I'm a superhero."

"Really?" Amber said, grinning.

"Oh yeah, I fly around saving people in distress. Turns out, though, I'm not impervious to punches. I bruise easily."

"I was going to say, you don't seem to be made of steel."

"Just my abs."

"You really had that hard of a time coming up with something?"

"Yes, I did."

Amber gave him a look.

"I needed some insight into the complex mind of a red-headed senior."

"Do you know what I'm thinking now?"

"You're thinking of saying something mean-spirited?"

"Possibly."

"Despite my initial laziness, I actually did all of the work myself, especially since Courtney told me she couldn't help and that I should do the work myself. I think you'll be quite pleased despite my initial hesitation to complete the task."

"OK, I'll see what you have up your sleeve."

The two teens dined at a local restaurant that filled most of its seats on a busy Saturday night.

"Too cold to do much outside yet, so everyone eats out this time of year," John commented as they watched people entering and exiting the restaurant.

"If no one was here, we'd be worried I guess," Amber responded. "So have you heard anything back from my college yet?"

"No, not yet. Wait a second, your college?"

"Yeah, Courtney and I already got in. But again, we have stellar credentials."

"You're saying my D grades don't impress them?"

"They must be weighing whether you're worthy enough to attend the same school as people like us."

"I'm sure that's it. They're probably just wondering why someone like me would consider them when Harvard and Yale is more my scene. They're probably just upset because my one request was to have a room right next to you two."

"I'm sure they were thrilled with that."

"Only bad thing is with a room so close by is that you'll be able to see a parade of people coming in and out of my room when I host a huge party."

"I can't envision you throwing a party."

"Yeah, you're right. My kind of a party is eating nachos while watching television."

"So, are you nervous about not knowing what you're doing next year?"

"Nah, not anymore. It will all work out. Maybe a month ago I'd be worried, but I'm not going to waste my time thinking about something that's out of my control. If I don't get in, I can find one of those seedy online schools that rip people off and give students suspect degrees."

"That could work for you. Diploma mills are cool."

"I'll be $500,000 in debt and no job. However, they'll sign up the students other schools reject, because, you know, I'm one of the warm bodies they're in need of."

"Nice. You can then seek revenge by working on Wall Street and ripping other people off."

"Absolutely, I can pay back the loans that way."

As the couple finished their dinner and got back in John's car, Amber voiced curiosity about what the evening held.

"This is so exciting, I can't wait to see what you have planned."

"Don't get your hopes up too much, it's not like I spent a thousand dollars for a hot air balloon ride or something."

"Wouldn't that be a bit cold on a night like tonight?"

"Possibly. And I'm a little skeptical of them after seeing that movie 'The Wizard of Oz.'"

"Haven't seen it. Just kidding."

John found parking on campus and walked with Amber along a dark sidewalk towards the fine arts building.

"OK, so can you tell me now?"

"I suppose I can. We're going to a college choir concert."

"Nice, how did you decide on this?"

"Well, I knew you liked music, so I tried to find something like that."

"Thanks, this is really nice," Amber responded as they entered the building.

John and Amber found seats in the middle of the performing arts center among a sparse audience. Between songs John looked over at Amber, trying to gauge her enjoyment level.

"So, is this going to be you next year?" John asked.

"I don't know. Not sure if I want to sing in college or just focus on classes. I'll have to see."

"I'm sure you'll do well if that's what you want to do."

"Thanks."

After an hour and a half, the concert ended, with students and adults filing out of the building.

"So, what did you think?" John asked, tentatively.

"It was great, thanks for taking me. You showed you could deliver under pressure and use some creativity."

"Don't make me do that too much, I might run out of ideas."

"Provided you get into Southeast Missouri Community College, are you going to do any extra activities?"

"Yeah, I think I'll study."

"Very funny, but seriously?"

"We'll see. I love basketball. I could play that forever, but obviously I won't be able to. I may give the coach of the team a call and see if he'd be interested in me."

"Yeah, you should do that if you want to keep playing. You played well the other night, maybe they'll see that you can play."

"Thanks, I'm sure my parents won't be thrilled with me playing. They're already skeptical of me playing in high school. They want me to just focus on academics and not fool around with such foolishness like basketball."

"Don't they want you to have some fun once in a while?"

"Apparently not."

"They'll just have to deal with it then. You should be able to do what you enjoy. It's not like it's hurting your grades or something."

"Yeah, I know. I don't get what bothers them about it, but it might be because they didn't do sports. My dad was in some academic clubs or something, and my mom took cooking classes I guess."

"That sounds exciting," Amber responded sarcastically.

"Yeah, I'm sure it was a real blast. It set up a lifelong love of reading the financial columns in the newspaper for my Dad. Something for him to do while my mom cooks the meals."

"You have a fascinating home life."

"It's a thrill a minute."

As John drove by the high school on the way home, he noticed three figures dressed in dark clothing sprinting across the parking lot. One of them threw something at the building.

"What in the world?" John asked.

"What?"

"Someone's trying to vandalize the school. I'm going to get a closer look."

John turned into the parking lot and drove toward a trio of vandals. As he got to the end of the building, he put the vehicle in park and got out of the car, running around the corner to hear voices.

"Hey, someone's here! Let's run."

Chapter 10

John recognized one of the faces peering back at him. He calmly got out his phone and recorded everything in front of him.

"Hey Matt, is this what you do with your Saturday evenings?" John enquired.

The group sprinted toward the back of the building and disappeared without responding to his question. John did not pursue them, content with identifying at least one person in the party.

John got back in the car, a bit out of breath from running.

"So?" Amber asked.

"Payback is rough," John said, grinning.

"What do you mean?"

"Our good friend Matt is at it again. A couple of his buddies were with him. I guess I'll go visit the principal on Monday morning to report it. I took some video with my phone, I'll see if it captured anything."

"So what were they throwing?"

"I think fruit and stuff. What do they think this is, a bad play from the 1400s?"

"He's everywhere apparently. Every time we go out it seems, he's there."

"In all fairness, I'm not sure he was at that wild party we saw the other week."

"True."

"We should actually call the police with the info."

"Good call."

John dialed and reported vandalism at the high school. He then put his car in drive and took off, not wanting to stay in a dark parking lot any longer with Matt lurking around. John pulled into Amber's driveway a few minutes later.

"Well, another interesting evening," John said.

"Yeah, it ended kind of weird, but you did well planning all of this," Amber responded.

John returned to his darkened house a few minutes later, his parents in bed at this hour. As he made his way through the kitchen, he saw a couple pieces of mail with his name on them, including one from Southeast Missouri Community College. John opened the college letter, wondering what news he was about to receive. He looked at the official-looking letter and began reading.

"Yes," John said quietly to himself.

The letter stated what John hoped to hear, that the school admitted him. He quickly texted Amber the good news, joking that he's now the girls' academic equal. She texted back a congratulatory message, as John headed toward his bedroom with a smile on his face, realizing he had at least one option for next fall.

The following morning, John sat at the kitchen table eating cereal as his parents readied for church that morning.

"So how did your date go last night?" John's mother asked.

"Good."

"Did you get the mail I left out for you?"

"Yeah, I got accepted by Southeast Missouri Community College."

"Nice, good to hear you're doing something valuable with your time other than getting in trouble on the basketball team."

John bit his lip, trying not to say what he thought. He

163

remained silent and continued to eat his cereal.

John's mother continued the discussion, much to his dismay.

"See, isn't life better when you get your priorities in order?"

John continued to eat his cereal.

"You don't have anything to say?"

"I'm not sure what you want me to say."

"Maybe recognize that your parents are right and that you should have listened to them."

"Yeah, because you can't play sports and care about academics at the same time."

"You spent too much time worrying about basketball."

"My grades have always been the same. Most parents come out to their kids' games, but you two are a no-show for most games. My senior year is almost done, and then it will be too late for you to attend anything."

"We've got other things to do than go to basketball games, John," his father chimed in.

"Nothing that's that important."

"We have responsibilities."

"Neither of you are working when I have games, so it's just stuff you want to do. You could take a few nights off from your book club and other stuff to see me play, but you don't."

"Basketball is not our thing, John," his dad continued.

"That shouldn't matter. Most parents support their kids' interests, and I'm sitting here trying to convince you to even show up."

John's parents remained silent for a few moments before John spoke.

"Look, I guess you can do what want, but I've been playing basketball forever and you've missed most of my games. I'm out of here in a few months, and then you won't have to go to anything of mine, so this was your opportunity."

"Let's not talk about it anymore," John's mom said, wanting to end the conversation.

Monday morning, John stopped by Don Harmon's classroom before bringing his video to the principal.

"John, you played a great game the other night!" Don said.

"Thanks."

"I can't believe you've been hiding these skills from us this long."

"I wish we were doing better as a team, but it's fun to play."

"You're definitely not part of the problem, so keep it up."

"Thanks, I'm glad you come out to the games, it's great having lots of fans there."

"Your parents must be proud of you doing so well."

"They don't actually go to many of my games. They kind of want to do other stuff."

"That's too bad. How's that college stuff going for you?"

"Good, I actually just got accepted to Southeast Missouri Community College."

"Wow, congrats!" Don replied. "This is a good week for you. I guess you deserve one after the year you've had."

"Thanks."

As John strolled through the hall, he spotted Amber. "Hey, how's my current and future classmate?"

"I'm great, but I don't know if I want you that close by, though in college. It kind of makes it harder to date other guys."

"Gee, thanks. I didn't know you had the tremendous urge to cheat."

"Why should I limit myself to just one person?"

"It's all about you isn't it? And what about my feelings?"

"Wait, you have feelings?"

"Sometimes. This one time I felt hungry."

Amber laughed. "In that case, I guess I'll have to allow you to go to my school."

"Well, that's a relief. Anyway, I'm off to the principal's office to show him my tape."

"Nice, I hope he enjoys it."

John walked into the Principal Charles' a few seconds later, feeling his usual nerves.

"Well, I happened to be in the right place at the right time," John explained. "Here's the video I took, in hopes of identifying the culprits. I know who Matt is, of course, but the other two I don't know."

"Thanks, let's have a look."

Mr. Charles leaned over his desk, peering at John's video.

"Well, I'll work with the police department to get to the bottom of this," the principal responded, digesting the contents of John's recording. "Make sure you hang on to that, the officers are looking into it. They left a mess on the side of our school walls and windows that's hard to clean up, so we'd like to find out who was involved. We'll definitely chat with Matt, he's been one of the more difficult students to deal with at the school."

"I just wish he'd stop the bullying. I'm sure he goes after a number of students, and it's a real pain to deal with."

"Yes, I remember our last chat," Principal Charles responded. "Thanks for stopping by and sharing the information, we appreciate it."

As John walked out of the office, Coach Thompson passed him in the hall and stopped.

"John, I've been meaning to talk with you."

"Yeah?"

"Yes, could you come on over to the office with me?"

"Sure."

As John entered the office, Coach Thompson sat behind his desk.

"I just wanted say that you've done a great job so far."

"Thanks."

"I know we haven't gotten the results we're looking for, but considering the situation you've done as well as you could. You've kept the offense going and haven't been selfish out there."

John smiled. "Did you expect me to be firing up jumpers every time I touched the ball?"

"No, but let's be honest, you were upset not to be on the floor, and players like that usually try to play for themselves."

"I've never wanted that," John responded. "I just wanted to be a part of the team and have some role, no matter how small, in the outcome of games. It's tough to do that riding the end of the bench and receiving ridicule from the starters."

Coach Thompson nodded before John continued.

"I've tried to talk to my teammates about team play, but obviously it's not working too well. Guys are talking about 'getting theirs' and not caring if they shoot into double teams."

"We'll be watching some film this week, and I'll point out the instances you're talking about to try to clean that up, but we only have the guys we have, and if they won't listen, we're kind of stuck until the other guys get back. How about this, though? I'll give you the floor tonight and you can address the team. Try to get some team unity going. How does that sound?"

"Sure, I'll do my best. Not sure if anyone wants to hear from me, though."

"They need to hear from you, and we need to be on the same page. So I take it the team is pretty fractured right now, huh?"

"Yeah, to say the least," John replied. "The suspended starters don't respect the guys playing for them, and we're not fans of them, so it's a bit crazy."

That afternoon at practice, Coach Thompson reminded them that three games remained before the regional tournament began and that the team had work to do. As practice began, John noticed the division between teammates, as the suspended group did not interact with the other players. The Leopards worked on their game plan for their next contest Tuesday against Central. They finished their season taking on East and South high schools. The Leopards would play the first two games on the road but would host South High to end the season.

As practice concluded, Coach Thompson called the team together.

"OK guys, this hasn't been a great practice. Not enough energy for a team that can win the conference title. I'm going to do something different and let one of our players address the team and I hope you will listen. When the postseason starts, everyone will be eligible to play and we will need a team effort. I've been impressed with John Zander's effort these last few weeks, and he has some things he wants to say. John, the floor is yours, and you have the last word."

John felt more nervous than in the middle of a big game. "I'm not a speech guy, but I'll get right to the point. If we want to do something big this year, we have to change our attitudes. My attitude was wrong this season, and I'm frustrated with some of our attitudes now. We need to find a way to treat each other better and respect each other. Some of us have been vicious to each other and it has to stop. If it doesn't, we won't win. It's that simple."

John took a second to look at each of his teammates and then looked at the suspended starting five. "Those of you who are suspended, you're looking down on everyone else. That's ridiculous, because you rely on those who start the game on the bench every game to give you a rest and play well. You guys have been arrogant and it needs to stop. Guys who are playing with me right now, we have to change. Everybody's trying to play for themselves and not doing what's best for the team, and that, ultimately, will hurt everyone. We need to play team ball. And guess what? You'll find you have better opportunities to make baskets when you aren't worried about forcing everything. You've got to hear me on this: stop worrying about how many points you're each scoring. Winning is what matters. If we keep doing this, coach will put all of us right back on the bench when the postseason starts and you'll have no excuses."

The gym remained silent, with many players keeping their heads down.

"Guys, we only get one shot at this. We have the talent to win a state title this year, but we have to figure things out. We still can win this conference and do well, but we've done a lot of things this season that should embarrass us. Instead of playing hard as a team, everyone's been concerned about themselves. I've been selfish, you've been selfish and we need to behave like a team instead of just a bunch of individuals trying to boost a stat line. We need to treat each other with respect and recognize that everyone has a part in this, or we won't go anywhere."

John looked around the gym and pointed to the banners.

"Do we want a banner up there, or are we going to be looking back years from now wondering how we messed this up? Are you willing to ruin this because of selfishness? We still have time to right the ship, but we need to do it right now. Who's in and who wants to keep the status quo? We have to ask ourselves what our goals are."

After a few seconds of silence, DeShaun Porter spoke. "John's right guys. Rob and I've only been on the team for a bit, and we can tell everyone doesn't like each other. We have a great team, and yet everybody's fighting for some reason."

Rob Dixon nodded his head in agreement. "We can do better."

Coach Thompson stood to the side, taking everything in and then walked over to the group.

"So what do you guys think about what John just said?"

Again, silence reigned.

"This is it, guys, if each one of us doesn't change, this team won't reach any of the goals you can and should reach this year," Coach Thompson stated. "It's completely up to you whether you want to change your ways and treat people the way you should or keep derailing our season with this fighting stuff."

Coach Thompson looked around and decided to challenge the guys.

"Seniors, I'm looking at you. What's it going to be Teyshaun? Rashad? How about you, Braden?"

The seniors just looked at each other without speaking.

"I have to say I'm disappointed," Coach Thompson concluded. "I really thought winning and a team-first philosophy was what you guys are about. And instead I've been breaking up fights half the season. Think about all this tonight, guys."

The locker room was unusually quiet as the players changed clothes and left for home. John trudged out to his vehicle, thankful no one in the locker room mocked him for his speech. John heard a voice as he opened his car door.

"Hey, you did good out there today," DeShaun said from a nearby vehicle. "Guys are gonna be disappointed if they don't go to state this year just because of some fighting."

"Thanks, man."

The following evening, the Leopards traveled to Central

High to play the second-to-last-place team in the conference. North's opponent knew this was a chance for a win and took it to the Leopards early. John started the game on the bench and sat next to the two sophomore call-ups.

"Dude, we can't lose to these guys," John said, leaning over to DeShaun.

"I know, they beat Lincoln twice and that's it," DeShaun responded.

"When we get out there, we better stick it to them."

"What do you mean 'we'?" Rob asked. "You'll be out there before us!"

"Be ready, you might be out there with me," John replied seriously.

A frustrated Coach Thompson called John over to the scorer's table just a few minutes into the game as the team's first substitute.

"Run point guard, John, we need to fix this right now," Coach Thompson explained.

John steadied the ship once he came into the game, running the plays without turning the ball over. He dished the ball inside to Sam Stevens and Dan Zimmerman, trying to get some baskets in the post. The Leopards rallied back by the end of the first quarter, tying the game 15-15.

"Guys, we need to take care of the ball," Coach Thompson shouted at the players in the huddle between quarters. "Let's continue getting the ball in the post where we've had success, and shooters be ready if they start double-teaming Sam and Dan."

John took the floor to begin the second quarter with Dominique Carter, Sam, Dan and Terrance White. After not scoring in the first quarter, John found himself open for a jumper shortly into the quarter and buried it, putting the Leopards up 19-17 over Central. He found teammates the rest of the quarter, as Dominique and Terrance began making open shots. North had the momentum at the end of the quarter, leading 29-25.

Coach Thompson praised the team at the half for their defensive efforts and team play on offense. The two sophomores even contributed in the first half. As the third quarter started, John began the half on the bench. North kept a slim lead throughout the quarter, taking a 37-35 advantage into the final quarter.

"John, you're going to be playing point guard for most of the fourth, OK?" Coach Thompson said, looking up from his dry-erase board.

John took the floor with the current group, which included Erick Samuels at forward. He hoped he would pass the ball instead of putting up bad shots. Shortly into the quarter, Erick received the ball in the post and immediately made a move to the basket. A second defender came over to help and a third rushed behind him. Erick, now surrounded by three defenders, jumped in the air trying to get off a short jumper. The ball clanged off the rim to a Central rebounder. At the next timeout, John stood in the huddle with his teammates and looked over at Erick.

"You've got three guys on you Erick and you still shot the ball. Pass it to someone who's open!"

Coach Thompson turned to face Erick. "We need to move the ball, and that's not at all the shot we want. Wait for something much better and move the ball."

Erick glared at John. "You not getting enough points, John? You want me to pass it to you, right?"

John stared at Erick.

Coach Thompson looked up from his kneeling position in the middle of the huddle. "Erick, have a seat. You won't be playing the rest of the way with that attitude. I'll be talking to you after the game."

Coach Thompson waved to Rob. "Come on over here, Rob. You're in for Erick."

With Rob in the game, the Leopards began moving the ball and cashed in, as the guards found holes in the defense and took the ball to the basket. John hit several jumpers from inside the three-point line, helping the Leopards to a 10-point lead with three minutes left. Central trimmed the lead with a couple three-pointers, but North hit its free throws down the stretch to win 61-52.

"How about that, Rob?" John said with a smile on his face as he headed toward the locker room.

Rob smiled back, as DeShaun ran up behind the two of them with a big grin on his face. "We're playing ball now, huh? John, man, you're doing a great job out there!"

"Thanks, DeShaun, you guys did well."

"Dude, I was in there for, like, a minute, but you were the court leader!"

As the players walked into the locker room, Braden sat at his locker and looked up at John.

"Enjoy your 15 minutes of fame, dude."

"So, you're not happy for the team doing well?" John responded.

"Yeah, like you care about the team. Where was that when you were rotting on the bench?"

"When was I angry about the team doing well? I just didn't like your attitude toward me. Keep up the bitterness, it really will do you well."

"Like I said, it will all be over for you in a few days."

"No, it won't. I showed what I can do and will continue to do my best. If I'm back on the bench, oh well. At least I won't go through life thinking I'm a hot shot."

John walked away and joined those who played alongside

him in the victory. He noticed the suspended starting five quietly sat in a corner of the locker room while everyone else celebrated the win. The team received more good news after discovering the team just one game behind them in the standings, West High, lost a close road game giving the Leopards a two-game lead.

On the bus, John chatted on the phone with Amber.

"Hey, congrats on the win," Amber said excitedly. "You guys are doing pretty well for having all backups in the game."

"Yeah, it's been good. We have a couple tough ones to go, but the last one is at home, so we'll see."

At home, John's parents informed him they planned to go to his final home game against South on Tuesday. They seemed to expect excitement from John upon this joyous announcement, but John didn't say much, thinking to himself "It's about time."

North's winning streak was short-lived, as the team struggled on the road against fourth-place East High. The East forwards overwhelmed the Leopards' backups, scoring at will in the post. The defense made it tough for John to get the ball inside, as the team only mustered tough shots. East won the game 60-45, the final score appearing closer than it was due to the East High coach inserting backups most of the fourth quarter after holding a 52-25 third quarter lead.

Several of the East players had words for John during the game, as he remembered bumping into them at the YMCA. "I told you we'd kick your butts," one East student said to John as he sat on the bench near the end of the game.

John just shook his head, ignoring his former YMCA opponent. He knew this was not the Leopards' best effort and better days may be ahead of them.

"Did they give us back the white flag we threw at them?"

Erick Samuels asked as he threw open the locker room door after the game.

"It's tough to remember since you gave it to them in the first quarter, Erick," Dan Zimmerman shot back at him.

"Guys, enough," John said. "Haven't we done enough fighting this season? We just need to keep getting better and try taking open shots."

For once, no one said anything back to him. John saw a few of the suspended starters snickering in the locker room, but it no longer bothered him. He knew his group had one more game left and that they might play better. As John left the locker room, Coach Thompson leaned up against a wall, looking unraveled after the tough loss.

"That was a thumping, huh John?"

"Yeah," John responded quietly.

"You've done everything we've asked."

"Thanks."

"I mean it, even tonight you scored eight points and kept everything running without a bunch of turnovers. Your teammates may not recognize it, but I do. It's not your fault for everything that's happening out there, so just keep doing what you're doing, and we'll be OK."

"I appreciate that."

Monday morning as John stood outside his locker chatting with Amber and Courtney, he spotted Braden and Stephanie arguing outside his locker. Braden shook his head and walked away, with Stephanie wiping away tears.

"I better go over there," John said, walking toward Stephanie.

Amber leaned over to Courtney, whispering to her what happened the last time John talked to her.

"Hey, everything OK?" John asked, as she looked up with red eyes. "I mean, relatively speaking."

"Does everything look OK?"

John remained silent, waiting for her to explain.

"I think we're done."

"That may not be the worst thing. You're too young to be miserable in a relationship. At least wait until you're older and then you can be miserable like some other elderly people."

"Very funny. At least you seem to be happy with Amber."

"I am, she's nice."

"Why can't Braden be nice?"

"I know it's none of my business, but if he doesn't treat you well, why stay? We're in high school, you could wait until college to meet guys."

"I'm wondering that myself."

"Well, if you need anything, let me know. I hope things get better."

"Thanks, John. You're a good guy."

"I don't always feel that way, but thanks."

As John sat at lunch that day, his friends wanted to know more about the conversation he had with Stephanie.

"Amber, are you jealous John was talking to another woman?" Courtney asked with a big grin on her face."

"Shut up."

"So John, did you ask her out at a time when you're not with Amber?"

"Wow! You really like to get after people, don't you Courtney?" John responded. "One of these days I'll get after you about something. For example, have you ever proven that you're not dating Matt the bully?"

"I am, and he's awesome."

"He's the strong, delinquent type, huh?"

"So John, Courtney and I are going to your game Tuesday night," Amber said.

"Cool, you'll get to see me play for the last time this season. I'm back on the bench come playoffs."

"But you're playing so well," Courtney stated.

"Yeah, well, the starters will be back, and there won't any playing time available for me."

"You never know what can happen," Amber replied.

John took a long look around the gym as he warmed up for Tuesday night's home game against fifth-place South High, realizing this may be his last chance to receive meaningful action in a game. He tried not to become nervous or feel pressure to play well. John thought about relaxing and having fun, despite that they needed to win the game to secure a conference title.

"Hey, let's go!" DeShaun said, slapping John's hand. "We've got a title to win."

"Absolutely, we've gotta have this one."

John began the game on the bench, but received game action just five minutes into the contest. Dominique and Terrance shot the ball well early, so John fed them the ball to get them as many shots as possible. At the end of the half, John did not have any shots, but the team led 39-38 due to solid shooting from the Leopards.

"One more half to go, team!" Coach Thompson shouted in the locker room. "We have to win this game to get the conference title and have a top seed in the regionals, so dig deep and find a way to get it done. We played well in the first half, but we've got to keep it up."

South made a run to start the third quarter, as John watched from the bench.

"Dude, we better not get too far behind," John told DeShaun, who sat next to him. He looked down the bench to gauge the team's mood. Most of John's teammates still did not say much to him, but no one was openly critical of him since he gave them his message on team unity. John wasn't sure what the team thought about what he said. They may not care about unity, but they didn't want to state that fact.

Amber and Courtney sat in the stands, as John scanned the crowd for his parents. They sat on one side of the gym, looking uncomfortable. He spotted a few people from the community he knew, including Don and Julie Harmon.

"What are you looking at?" DeShaun asked.

"Oh, just seeing who's at the game," John said. "My parents rarely come to my games, so it's surprising they're here."

"Really?" Rob asked. "Mine go to all my games, even like when I rarely play like tonight."

"That's the way it goes," John said. "I think they came tonight just so people wouldn't look at them like they're crazy when they tell them they hadn't seen any of my games. They're not basketball people."

Coach Thompson interrupted John's conversation by summoning him to the scorer's table to give Darnell a break. As John ran out onto the floor, he looked up at the scoreboard reading 52-49 in favor of South. Several North turnovers in a row led to a 56-49 South advantage.

"Come on!" John shouted, trying to fire up the team after a South layup. "Let's go, right now!"

John dribbled up court and fired a pass to Terrance who used a pick to get open at the three-point line. He sank the shot as the crowd roared. The team walked over to Coach Thompson at the end of the quarter, with South up 58-55.

John tried to fire the guys up as they walked off the court. "We've got to pick it up, guys. We can beat this team, they're not that good."

John's teammates did not respond, and instead wore weary expressions on their faces. John started the quarter sitting next to his coach as the game went back and forth.

"So what are you seeing out there, John?" Coach Thompson asked.

"We just need to play with more energy," John replied. "It seems like guys are tired, and I'm not sure why.

"OK, I'll send you in with the two sophomores and see what happens. If they start to make a run, though, I'll have to go back to this current group."

With seven minutes left in the game and the Leopards trailing 69-65, John and a new group of teammates entered the game.

"We need lots of energy guys, and we've got to stay within striking distance, so we have to start playing right now."

John pushed the ball up the floor on their first possession and tossed the ball to DeShaun, who made a move to the basket before dumping a pass to Rob underneath the basket. Rob went straight up and put in a layup to bring the team within two. After several defensive stops, North took the lead on baskets by Juan and DeShaun. As John dribbled the ball up the court, he noticed the defender sinking below the three-point line. John walked the ball up to the line and quickly fired a long ball, sinking the shot to give North a 74-69 lead with four minutes to go.

John pumped his fist as another five players entered the game for North. He took a seat as he hoped the next group could hold onto the lead. South evened the game at 76 with one minute left, as Coach Thompson surprised the team by summoning John and four of those sitting with him to the scorer's table.

"I can't believe we're actually going back in," DeShaun said as they sat on the floor, waiting for more court time.

"We did get the team the lead just a couple minutes ago, but yeah, I'm surprised he didn't stick with the group that's always out there at the end of games," John replied. "We better get it done."

When the next five entered the game, the final minute showcased stiff defense, with neither team wanting to give up a basket. North called a timeout with 20 seconds left and possession of the ball.

"I want crisp ball movement, looking for the open shot," Coach Thompson implored the team. "None of this one-on-one stuff. Keep an eye on the clock and make sure we not only get a shot off, but get a good one. Got it?"

The team nodded as they walked back onto the court.

"Don't let the ball stick in your hands. Let's get a great shot and beat these guys!"

John dribbled down the court and passed the ball quickly to DeShaun, who quickly passed the ball back to him against South's zone defense. John fired a pass to the other guard, Juan, who couldn't find an opening in the defense and passed it back to John, who saw the scoreboard winding down. He caught the ball and drove into the lane, before passing the ball to DeShaun, who sunk below the three-point line. DeShaun caught the ball and took the shot, draining it with two seconds left.

South quickly called a timeout, as the crowd went wild. John ran over to congratulate DeShaun.

"That's what I'm talking about, DeShaun!"

"Nice pass, dude, all the defenders went with you, leaving me open."

"That's how you beat a zone, fellas," Coach Thompson yelled, before quickly shifting the conversation to defense.

As the Leopards set up their defense to make one final stop, John reminded the team not to give up any long passes and that under no circumstances should they commit a foul. The defense did just that, as South was forced to make a pass to half court, where their guard turned and heaved the ball toward the rim as the clock expired. The shot was off target and short, as the Leopards sprinted off the court to celebrate.

John took a moment to look at the cheering crowd and teammates jumping around to congratulate each other. He wondered if this was the best feeling the team would have all season or if the best was still to arrive.

Chapter 11

The next few moments for John felt like a blur as fans rushed onto the court to greet the overjoyed players.

"Conference champions, man!" Rob Dixon shouted at John, as they slapped hands.

"You did great work out there, Rob!"

"Thanks, we found a way to get it done."

John looked over at the group of starters wearing warm-up suits standing at the side of the court. They seemed to be the least excited group on the court. After talking with his parents and friends, John returned to the locker room where Coach Thompson addressed the team.

"I just want to congratulate you guys on a true team effort to win this conference," Coach Thompson began. "Despite the many issues this year, everyone on this team contributed to this title. Those of you who started for most of the season put us in this position with your play, and then everyone else on the team stepped up to finish the job. This was a great win tonight. We beat one of the better teams in the conference, which is incredible considering we're without our starting five. This win will probably get us a one seed in the playoffs, so we can look forward to more home games."

Those who played in the game were all smiles in the locker room, congratulating each other on the win.

DeShaun sat next to John as they readied to leave the locker room. "So, do you think this is it? Are we back to the bench?"

"Yeah, probably, but hey, look at all the experience you got this season. You've still got two more years to go. You're gonna be great if you keep working hard. The best is still to come for you."

"I guess it kind of sucks to be you right now, then, right? You're all done after this season."

"It's OK, these last few weeks have been the most fun I've had in basketball in a long time. Whatever happens after tonight will be OK. I did the best I could, I got some playing time that I never thought I'd get and I held up OK out there, so I've got nothing to complain about."

"You don't care if you rot on the bench in the playoffs?"

"Of course I'd like to play and help the team win, but you know how it is with the starters returning. Things will likely go back to what they were before their suspensions. I hope the starters treat everyone better, but I'm not holding my breath."

A few minutes later, John returned home. His parents readied to retire for the evening, but saw John head through the kitchen on the way to his room.

"John, you did a nice job out there tonight," his Dad remarked.

"Thanks."

"Do you always get to be in the game that much?"

"You could have shown up at the other games to find out."

As John's parents turned out the lights in the house after they returned home, John plopped on the couch, watching television in the dark.

"So this is as good as life gets, huh?" John wondered to himself. "My five minutes of fun is now over and I have to get back to the real world."

Between Wednesday classes, John chatted with Amber and Courtney in the hall as students weaved their way to classes. An elbow caught John on the arm by someone passing by.

"So you think you're some kind of hot shot now, huh?"

John recognized the voice of his favorite bully, Matt.

"I've never been a hot shot and I'm not one now, but at least I'm not a bully," John responded.

"Yeah, I'll bet you think you're pretty good right now, so I'm going to have to teach you a lesson."

"What is wrong with you, man? Are you even supposed to be in the building? Aren't you suspended?"

"I can be wherever I want."

"I'm not bothering you, why do you keep looking for me? You've got issues man, why don't you get help?"

John turned to Courtney and Amber. "You better get to class, I'll see you later."

As the girls began walking, John whispered to Amber. "Record what happens next on your phone."

Just then John's teammates walked by, including Rob Dixon, DeShaun, Juan Hernandez and Dan Zimmerman.

John turned to his teammates. "Hey guys, Mr. bully here thinks I'm a hot shot."

"Really?" DeShaun asked.

"This is the guy I told you about who was throwing stuff at the school the other day and harasses my friends and I all the time. He's got a lot of time on his hands. Hey Matt, what do you think of these guys?"

Matt looked over at the guys and decided not to antagonize them. "I was about to beat up your friend John here to make sure he doesn't get too big of a head."

"You're not going to do that to our teammate," Juan said quietly.

Matt flashed an angry look at Juan. "It doesn't matter what you think, I'm going to do what I want."

At this point, most students were in their classrooms, but John saw Amber holding up her phone off the side.

"Get lost, Matt, or I'll report you once again the principal."

"You're going to tell on me? Maybe I'll make sure you don't talk."

With that, Matt threw a punch as John got his arms over his face. John's teammates tackled Matt immediately. The bully began swinging his fists wildly trying to hit as many guys as he could. As Matt landed on the floor, Matt landed a punch on Juan, but John threw a fist that sent him sprawling. Matt grabbed his jaw in pain, pulled himself off the floor and walked away.

"Dude, what was that all about?" DeShaun asked.

"He's been going after people all school year and obviously has some problems," John explained. "I saw him picking on a freshman one day and asked him to stop. Since then, he's been going after me."

"I got it all on video," Amber interjected.

"Good," John stated. "Let's take it to the principal. I think Matt finally may be getting some consequences."

The whole group went down to the principal's office and showed him the video, complete with Matt punching Juan.

"Your jaw may be sore for a while, Juan," John said with a smile.

"At least he hits like a sissy," Juan replied. "That could have hurt if he actually put some muscle behind it."

As John handed his teacher a principal-signed pass to return to class, he heard the Matt being summoned to the office over the speaker system.

"Did he beat you up again, John?" a classmate muttered as John found his desk.

"Do I look beat up?"

"I don't know, maybe he punched you in the stomach."

A few classmates snickered as John threw his books down on the desk.

"Yeah, that's likely. If you want me beat up, you'll have to do the job yourself."

"Basketball players are punks," the classmate responded.

John just ignored the last comment and tried to focus on the class.

Before practice started later that day, John and those involved in the fight talked to coach about what happened, hoping they would not incur the coach's wrath despite the fact they did not start the brawl. The Leopards, a one-seed, prepared to play last-place Lincoln on Friday evening.

Coach Thompson thanked them for letting him know what happened and did not scold them, much to John's appreciation.

"Well, he took that well," John told Juan with a smile.

"Yeah, well I got punched so it couldn't have gotten worse than that," Juan responded.

"Good point."

John and his fellow reserves went back to their usual roles with the starters back in action. He stood on the sidelines with his teammates as they watched the first group run plays. When the team began scrimmaging, John remained on the bench with the other four remaining players. The two sophomores remained with the team to fill the roster out to 15 for the playoffs.

"Looks like we're back to normal," John joked with the others.

"Yeah, back to being a scrub," Juan added.

Friday night, John sat on the end of the bench among 10 others as the Leopards quickly rolled over their opponent. North held a 30-point 45-15 lead at halftime, as the starters displayed confidence and a spring in their step returning from suspension. The starting group laughed and gave each other high-fives in the locker room at the half, knowing the game was over.

186

"Well, looks like we'll be getting some playing time soon," Erick Samuels said quietly, as the backups displayed more reserved behavior in the locker room.

"What? So you can shoot it every time you touch it, Erick?" Juan responded.

"He's not a selfish player, he just wants what's his and will leave everyone else the scraps," Dan Zimmerman joked.

"You're just jealous of my game," Erick fired back.

The guys just laughed, trying to refrain from further insults.

As the fourth quarter started, John's group entered the game. The first five guys off the bench played most of the third quarter, building a 70-30 advantage. John dished passes and tried to get his teammates involved, while limiting turnovers. The Leopards continued to roll, as John had five points and everyone on the team scored to make the scorer's book by the end of the night. North held a 91-42 advantage as the final horn sounded, as the team moved on to the second round of the playoffs.

The following Tuesday, North hosted four-seed East High, a tougher opponent than Lincoln. The starters got off to a slow start, as East grabbed a 16-12 first-quarter lead.

"Yeah, maybe rolling over Lincoln wasn't such a good thing for their egos," John commented as Coach Thompson yelled at the team between quarters.

"Nothing's going to be that easy in the playoffs," Juan responded.

"No room for error now," John responded. "We have to bring it every night or season's over. I feel like I'm ready to go, but I guess that doesn't matter. How about you guys?"

"I had some French fries before the game, so I'm good," Erick said.

"You'd eat them on the darn bench if you could," Terrance said from several players down on the bench.

"You can't criticize me from that far away man!" Erick said. "You weren't even supposed to be hearing this."

John tuned out his teammates and looked up in the stands. His parents did not come out to this game but did show up at the first playoff game. John spotted Amber and Courtney sitting together near the top of the bleachers. He tried not to think about the fact the season was almost over or whether he would miss playing for the team.

North trailed 31-29 after a half of uninspired basketball. The starters looked flat, missing shots and lacking energy. Coach Thompson performed his usual halftime antics, voicing his displeasure with the team's play.

"I'll give his act a seven out of 10," Terrence whispered. "He's not perspiring as much as usual."

Erick tried to hold back laughter as the coach continued. John hoped the coach did not see the jokesters, or they would remain on the bench.

Halfway through the third quarter, Coach Thompson summoned several backups to the scorer's table, including John. As the group checked in, the scoreboard read 43-40 in favor of the road team. John dribbled the ball up the court and drove through the defense toward the basket, kicking the ball out to Terrance in the corner, who dropped in a three-pointer to tie the game and ignite the crowd. The fans had remained quiet most of the game but now had something to cheer about. East turned the ball over a few seconds later, and Dan heaved a pass down the court to Juan, who laid the ball in to give North the lead, 45-43. By the end of the quarter, North held a 54-50 advantage.

"I'm staying with this group, gentlemen, since it seems to be working," Coach Thompson explained on the bench.

John looked over at Juan, Dan, Terrence and Sam. He knew they had to play well to stay in the game and finish the job.

"Hey, let's keep it up," John instructed the team as they walked back onto the court. "Keep up the intensity, and let's finish these guys!"

The Leopards pulled away quickly, as the North post players found room to work inside and scored several baskets underneath. John hit a jumper near the elbow and often found his guards spotting up for shots. The starting group entered the game halfway through the quarter, with the Leopards ahead 62-47. When the final horn sounded, North held a 72-62 advantage. Coach Thompson praised the backups in the locker room, complementing the group on their team play and ball movement.

Coach Thompson found John after he left the locker room.

"John, nice job out there."

"Thanks coach."

"You're really helping this team. I can't believe how much you've improved since your suspension. What happened?"

"Just a lot of work on my own. I just wanted to be my best."

"Well, you're going to play an important role in us accomplishing what we want this season."

"Thanks."

The Leopards played for the regional title Friday evening and had two days to prepare for the two-seed West High, the only other team remaining in the playoffs from its conference. John grabbed his books from his locker Wednesday to head to class Stephanie walked by.

"Hey, so I broke up with Braden," Stephanie said without a greeting.

"I'm sorry to hear that," John said.

"Really? I thought you'd be happy."

"Why? I don't hate him."

"Well, you two don't get along anymore."

"No, we haven't been friends for a while, but that doesn't

mean I'm wishing him ill. I just wish he'd treat people better."

"He's just doesn't seem to care about me. All he cares about is himself."

"That stinks. I wouldn't worry about it, you have your entire college career to meet new people and find those who want to be around you. Everything will be OK."

"Are things OK with you?"

"Yeah, I'm looking forward to being done here so I can start something new. Get out of this city for a bit."

"So you're looking for a fresh start too, huh?"

"Just depends on the day I guess. Last night I did OK playing basketball, and that was fun. I'm trying harder not to think about the negative things, like Braden and that crazy bully who keeps causing trouble. I'm trying to focus on positives, like basketball and my friends. It'll all be OK."

"I just wonder what I'm going to do now. I spent all this time with him, and now I've got to make changes."

"You'll be OK. Just hang out with your friends like always."

John looked at Stephanie, who was fighting back tears.

"Listen to me, Stephanie, you've got a great future ahead of you. You are smart enough to tell when something isn't working, and you will do well in college next year. You can choose any life you want, you just have to choose good friends who will respect you. If you can do that, you'll have a good start."

"Thanks John, I'll see you around. I hope you keep winning in basketball."

"I hope so too, but if we don't, it's not the end of the world."

At lunch that day, John looked across the cafeteria to see Stephanie laughing with a group of friends. He smiled, realizing teenage crises often dissolve quickly.

"John, you still with us," Courtney said, as John looked

back at the girls, whose chatter he was ignoring.

"Yeah, sorry."

"You OK today?" Amber asked.

"Yeah, definitely."

"So why didn't your parents make it to the game last night?"

"I don't know, they were having dinner with friends."

"Your parents will literally make up any excuse to miss your games, won't they?"

"Not a big deal, even if they make it to games, it's not going to impress me at this point. I guess I've just realized they are who they are. They don't like basketball, and that's that."

"But shouldn't they support you and what you're interested in?" Courtney asked.

"Maybe, but it's too late for that."

The Leopards traveled out of town to a neutral site to play West Friday evening. North practiced well Wednesday and Thursday and felt ready to take on a tough team. John took a few reps with the second team, but wasn't sure how much he'd play.

North got off to a quick start, taking a 10-4 lead. John sat near the end of the bench with the third team and saw Amber and Courtney sitting across the gym. He felt good knowing at least a couple of his friends supported him and the team. Late in the second quarter, John entered the game and joined four of the starters. Facing a zone defense, John stationed himself on a wing with Rashad Alexander at the top of the three-point line.

John saw Braden come open on the wing and lobbed the ball to him. A defender went around him and knocked the ball out of his hands and dove on the loose ball before passing to a teammate. The Leopards called timeout with a 31-27 lead with under a minute to go in the half.

"You've got fight for that!" John said to Braden as they huddled around Coach Thompson.

Braden did not respond, realizing he should have come down with the ball.

"Yeah, we've got to be tougher," Coach Thompson explained to the team. "Some of you guys are letting West out-hustle you. We need to be the aggressor if we want the title."

In the third quarter, the Leopards built a 10-point lead, as the starters scored baskets on break-away baskets. West battled back in the fourth quarter and trailed 59-57 with 30 seconds left. Much to John's surprise, Coach Thompson summoned him over to the scorer's table as West called a timeout.

"You're in for Teyshaun," Coach Thompson explained. "Help us finish strong."

John nodded as he took the floor. West had the ball, but after a tipped pass the Leopards started another fast break. John followed the ball as Rashad lobbed the ball to Braden under the basket. Braden went up for the layup but put too much on the shot, which rolled off the rim. The defender tipped the ball back toward the free-throw line. John picked up the ball, took a couple dribbles and tossed a floater toward the rim, sinking the shot for his first basket of the day.

The crowd roared as North held a 61-57 lead with 10 seconds to go. The defense held kept West from scoring and won the game as fans cheered the Leopards.

"Two more games until state!" Erick Samuels shouted to the team as they congratulated each other.

DeShaun approached John with a smile. "You're clutch, man."

"Right place at the right time I guess," John responded.

"Does Braden get the assist on that shot?" Rob asked wryly.

"That was a choke job right there," DeShaun added.

After hoisting the trophy and posing for photos, the team returned to the locker room in a celebratory mood. Despite the victories, starters and backups celebrated separately in different spots of the locker room.

John happened to leave the locker room at the same time as Braden, who nervously looked at him as they went for the door. John looked at him and just shook his head as he walked in the opposite direction, looking for his friends.

"You did it again!" Amber exclaimed as John approached her and Courtney outside the gym. "You play really well."

"Thanks, we've got two more to go to get to state. That's our only goal."

"You really want to make it to state, don't you?" Courtney asked.

"Yeah, this team can get there. We just have to play our best. Not sure if that will happen the way our team is fractured, but I hope we can."

"You guys have such a weird team," Amber commented. "Nobody likes each other."

"I know, it's like two separate groups all the time, and even the backups didn't like me most of the season. That's definitely not the mark of a good team, but somehow we're winning."

"Who do you play next?" Courtney asked.

"Not sure yet, let me check."

John scrolled through a high-school basketball Web site to find scores from that evening's game.

"Looks like Smith High. They won tonight by a couple of points tonight."

"What's their record?"

"20-3. We're playing in town, though, over at West High. We'll sort of have home court advantage."

John spent Sunday evening working out at the YMCA,

trying to get in as much practice to be ready for Thursday's game. If they won, they'd play Saturday afternoon for the sectional title game.

Monday morning, Principal Charles found John in the hallway.

"Just wanted to let you know Matt has been suspended from school for another week because of that incident the other day. In light of his other offenses, I thought this punishment is fair. Hopefully this will help discourage him from further violence."

"We'll see. Thanks for your help in all of this. He's made life miserable for me and some of my friends this year. He seems to always show up at different places, and then he just starts harassing us. I don't get it."

"He's had a tough life so far," Principal Charles stated. "That's all I can say. If you knew the situation, you'd realize how he might be prone to this kind of stuff."

"Yeah, I'm sure I would. It's just not fun to deal with right now, and I'm not sure he'll ever change his behavior."

After an exhausting basketball practice in which Coach Thompson put the Leopards through conditioning drills, John pulled into the garage. As he did, he noticed someone wandering up his driveway and up to his vehicle.

"Open up the door, John, I've got a gift for you," a familiar voice echoed.

"Great," John thought to himself.

Matt walked up to John's window, but he slid out the passenger side door. Just before he slid out he dial 911 and stated his address as he left the vehicle.

"Hey Matt, you bored not being at school today?"

"Time for you to pay."

"For what?"

Matt just lunged at him as John tried circling the vehicle.

194

"You're a real wimp running away from me like this," Matt snarled at him. "You got me suspended and now you're going to get beat up."

"You brought that on yourself, and what do you think this is going to get you?"

"You won't say anything or you'll get more of this."

"You're delusional, dude."

John stood near the hood of the car at the back of the garage.

"You want me? Here I am."

Matt growled and ran at him. As he approached, John stepped to the side and grabbed hold of him, pushing Matt headfirst into the hood of the car. Matt's face hit the hood as John pushed down. John then grabbed him again by the coat and pulled him back, throwing him into the garage wall.

"You done, Matt?"

Matt looked up, blood oozing from his nose. He touched his bloody nose and then looked up at John.

"No, we're not done."

John decided he better not push is luck and leaped over the hood of his now dented hood and scurried to the side door where he entered his house and locked the door behind him. He then heard an enraged Matt try to break down the door leading into his kitchen.

"Shoot!" John said, backing away.

"What's going on?" his mother asked, walking into the kitchen.

"Police are on the way, it's a bully from school who showed up. I need something to hit with."

John quickly found a baseball hat and opened the side door. Matt had given up trying to break it and was instead yelling. As soon as John opened the door, Matt stepped toward him. John swung at Matt's knees and heard him grunt as he connected across his knee caps.

"Aaahhh!" Matt cried.

A few moments later police arrived at John's home as Matt lay in pain in John's garage.

John ran out to greet them and explained the situation.

Officers carried away a still-angry Matt who yelled at John as they placed him in the squad car.

After John talked with officers for a few minutes to detail the events, John walked over to his parents, who stood in the driveway.

"Wow! I didn't expect that tonight," John said, walking back into the house.

After explaining what happened over dinner, John called Amber to tell her the tale.

"Maybe they can make a movie out of it," John joked. "'The Bully Who Wouldn't Quit,' or 'Desperate Cries of a Lonely Bully.' What do you think?"

"I don't know," Amber said with a smile. "Who would play you?"

"Somebody awesome I'm sure. It would probably be a 30-year-old who has extensive martial arts training. Maybe it would turn into something that's very loosely based on a true story. As long as I get money out of it, I don't care."

The next morning, the story circulated throughout North High as John went about his day. As he ate lunch with Amber and Courtney, a humorous male student walked by their table.

"Hey man, I have a couple of people I'd like you to break their kneecaps for me."

"They owe you some money?"

"Actually I owe them money. This way maybe they'll forget about it."

"I don't think you could afford my services then."

John figured this was not the last he would hear about the incident. At practice that evening, his fellow backups surrounded him while he sat, putting on his shoes.

"Gentlemen, you'll have to refer all questions to my media advisor."

"What happened, did he attack you?" Darnell asked.

"Yeah, the dude showed up at my house. He was mad because he got suspended again. I guess he didn't want to risk losing his 4.0 with all those missed classes."

Erick Samuels blinked his eyes. "So wait, he tries to beat you up and then when he gets in trouble for trying to beat you up, he seeks revenge by trying to beat you up?"

"OK, so maybe he doesn't have a 4.0."

"So what's he going to do once he gets in trouble for this?" Erick continued.

"He'll have to take it up a notch and kill me I suppose."

"So is he going to be doing hard time?"

"I don't know about that."

When Tuesday morning rolled around, John found out some details of his tormentor's arrest. The principal and an officer knocked on his classroom door, asking for his presence. The class snickered as he grabbed his backpack to leave.

John smiled as he made his way to the door of the suddenly-silent room. "Huh, so I guess forgery is a felony."

Everyone laughed, excluding the teacher, who only managed a smirk while waiting to resume the lesson.

During John's brief meeting, he learned Matt would soon face an expulsion hearing and face charges. John felt confident that Matt was done bothering him unless he wanted to go get in even bigger trouble.

"So you're sure Matt's not sitting somewhere sharpening knives with your name on it?" Courtney asked at lunch.

"No, it would cost a lot of money to have that much

engraving done," John replied.

"I didn't mean literally knives with your name on it, goofball!"

"Oh!" John said jokingly.

"So you ready for the big game Thursday?" Amber asked.

"We've had a couple good practices so far. I try not to think about it too much. I don't want to get too nervous. I may not play much anyway."

"Whatever, you've played well in the other playoff games," Courtney said.

"I just don't want to count on it, or else I might be disappointed. I have no idea what the coach's thinking most of the time."

"He doesn't tell you how much you'll be playing?" Amber asked.

"No, of course not. He can't promise anything, and I know that. It just depends on how the game's going. It's probably worked to my advantage sometimes, because he probably planned to take me out but didn't if I was playing well."

"You'll do well out there," Amber encouraged him. "Just don't get nervous."

John tried to remember that as his team lined up in the hall outside the West High gym Thursday evening, waiting to run onto the floor to the sounds of cheering fans at a sold-out event. John thought of Courtney and Amber in the stands, as well as his parents who agreed to attend the game despite the fact they'd have the misery of attending yet another game two days later if they won. The Smith High squad entered the gym first to strong applause before the Leopards got the go-ahead to run in.

"Let's go guys, go get-em!" Coach Thompson shouted as the team sprinted into the gym.

John felt as amped-up as ever and maintained a razor-focus

on every warm-up shot he took. As he took a seat on the bench after the national anthem, he turned to Juan who sat next to him.

"I'm kind of glad to not be starting. This gives me time to calm down. I'm too amped up."

"I would be if I thought I was playing, but I doubt that's going to happen."

"Yeah, I'm not sure if I will either. We'll see how it goes. You have to admit this is a cool game to attend though, huh?"

"Yeah, for sure. I wasn't positive we'd get this far with the way things were going this season, but we have the talent to do this."

The Leopards and their opponent seemed equally matched to start the game and played to a 10-10 tie to end the first quarter. Both teams seemed nervous and missed shots, keeping it a low-scoring affair. Coach Thompson only played two backups to start the game, so John figured he may use the bench less than normal to win the game.

"He's going to burn the guys out the way we're going now," Erick said, frustratingly.

John nodded. "Yeah, why change the formula now? Everyone played well the last few games. If we win, we'll have to play again in two days. We'll need some subs in that game, too."

The starters looked winded as they went into the locker room, trailing 25-20. Coach Thompson talked to the team about taking better shots and moving the ball.

"Yeah, well everybody wants to be the hero and no one wants to pass," Juan muttered the Leopards took the floor.

"We'll see if he starts putting guys in," John responded.

John was surprised when his coach put in the entire second unit mid-way through the third quarter.

"You're next, Juan," John joked.

"What about me?" DeShaun asked with a smile.

"He's saving you for the game-winner of course!"

"Why aren't you in, John?" Rob Dixon asked. "You were clutch this year."

"I don't know. Not gonna worry about it. If it had been earlier this year, I would have been mad. As long as we win, I'm good."

John turned to the guys with a sly smile on his face. "If we lose, I'm gonna be mad. Just kidding."

The four guys who hadn't played yet in the game laughed. Those in the game were not finding much humor as they trailed 45-35 heading into the fourth quarter. Several starters had trouble making shots, leading to the current deficit.

"We better make a run or we're done," DeShaun stated as the fourth quarter started.

Coach Thompson just finished a fiery speech to ready the troops for one final push. Two minutes into the quarter, the coach summoned John and Juan over to the scorer's table.

"I want Juan running point and you at shooting guard. You're in for Teyshaun and Rashad."

"Huh, didn't see that coming," Juan said calmly.

"Just don't turn it over," John said, smiling.

The Leopards still trailed by 10 in a scoreless fourth quarter when they entered the game, but Braden hit a short jumper on the first possession after John entered the game, and Juan tracked down a rebound and tossed the ball ahead to John, who threw it to a sprinting Joe Anthony. He finished the play with a layup to cut the lead to six. The crowd roared, sensing momentum.

Smith quickly called a timeout, but the Leopards' fans who made the trip across town to West High's gym continued cheering. Smith played a tough man-to-man defense, making open shots difficult to find. John held the ball on a wing as

Juan curled around a pick at the top of the three-point line. He threw a hard pass his way. Juan caught the ball in rhythm and fired a three-pointer that found the bottom of the net. The crowd cheered as John pumped his fist with excitement, clapping his hands on the way down the court.

"Here we go, let's keep it up!" John encouraged his teammates. North trailed by two just a few minutes later, but the same group continued to stay on the court with five minutes left. The Leopards secured a rebound and set up their offense on the other side of the court. Braden drew a double team after catching Juan's pass in the post, but he kicked it back to John. He took one dribble and fired his first shot of the game, a jumper from a few feet inside the three-point line. The ball went through to tie the game at 51.

"Yeah, that's how it's done!" Juan shouted at John, as he hustled back on defense.

At the next timeout, Coach Thompson gave high-fives to Juan and John, who then both took a seat on the bench as the starting guards re-entered the game. John looked at Rashad and Teyshaun as they walked by.

"Better win it, guys."

North then grabbed the lead, as Braden and Joe both scored baskets from the post as the crowd roared. Smith players seemed flustered by the baskets and missed jumpers. A bank shot from DaVonte put the Leopards up 57-51 with under a minute to go. By the time Smith scored, they began fouling to keep the clock from running out. North fans rose to their feet, sensing victory. The Leopards did not disappoint, making enough free throws to win the game 60-56.

"One more game!" Juan exclaimed as the players made their way to way to shake hands with their opponents.

"This is pretty cool," John responded. "It was a tough one, but we did it."

"We've only got a day and half before the next game," Coach Thompson warned the players in the locker room. "We haven't accomplished what we wanted to yet, but we just got one step closer. Let's work hard in practice tomorrow and then be ready for another big game."

At lunch the next day, John sat with his friends trying to forget about the pressure of the next day's game.

"At this time tomorrow, you'll be ready to play for the chance at state, that's pretty cool." Courtney stated.

"I know," John said with a smile. "We gotta win it. Last year we couldn't make it this far, so this has to be our time."

"You ever going to patch things up with Braden?" Amber asked.

"I don't think that's going to happen," John said. "We're almost done with high school, and it doesn't really matter anyway. After all that's happened, it would be tough to be buds again. He'll have to learn some lessons on his own, just like I had to."

John looked over his shoulder to see Stephanie walking to his table.

"May I grab a seat?"

"Of course," John said, pulling a chair out.

"I just wanted to thank you for talking to me this semester. You didn't have to do that, especially when Braden was a jerk to you."

"Oh, I didn't do much. You've had a tough time."

"I think I'm finally over everything. It also didn't hurt that I got into the college that I wanted."

"Oh, congrats!" Courtney said.

"Yeah, that's great," John added.

"It's out of state, but that might be good for me."

"Yeah, just find good people to hang with, and you'll do well. You can do whatever you want for a career."

"Well I just wanted to thank you again. I try talking to my friends, but they don't always like the whole listening thing so much."

"Yeah, anytime."

Stephanie got up from the table and walked away.

"Wow, I didn't realize you were such an inspiration to mankind, John!" Courtney said with a smile.

"What can I say? I have a big heart and a big ear."

"And an enormous ego."

"And I'd like to keep it growing like a tree."

"You know, trees fall sometimes," Amber added.

"And some stand for generations, looming over everyone."

"This analogy is getting out of hand," Courtney said.

As they talked, Steve walked by.

"Hey Steve, come over here a minute," John said. "I haven't seen you in a while."

Steve timidly walked over to the table.

"How have you been?"

"Good, sorry I haven't talked to you a while. Been busy with classes and everything. Hey, no one's bullied me in a long time. I guess you're a good bodyguard."

"It's my physique."

"Well good luck in tomorrow's game. That's pretty cool you're playing well and everything. I went to one of the playoff games. You were awesome."

"Thanks. Good talking to you."

As John walked through his house after practice evening, his mother stopped him.

"Hey John, Don Harmon wants to stop by in a bit and talk to you."

"OK, cool."

Later that evening, John answered a knock on the door.

"Hey Don, how are you?"

"I'm good John, just wanted to chat. We haven't had a chance to talk much recently."

The two settled into the living room, and John's parents soon joined them.

"So you got accepted into Southeast Missouri Community College?" Don said.

"Yeah, how about that."

"Were Courtney and Amber the reason for that decision?"

"It certainly didn't hurt!"

Don laughed, while John's parents did not find the humor in his comment.

"John, what I really wanted to stop by for was to let you know how much I admire what you've done recently. It's not easy to admit a mistake and then make changes. You did. I've talked to some of your bench mates, and they say nice things about you. This is going to help you for the future."

"Thanks."

Don turned to John's parents.

"You should be proud of him. He picked up the pieces, and now he's doing well."

"Well, he's doing what he should have been doing all along."

"Maybe so, but it's important to acknowledge progress. We all mess up, but when we try to make it right, then it's a great thing."

John's parents did not respond.

Don got up to leave a few minutes later.

"John, you're doing great. Keep up the hard work, and good luck tomorrow. I'm looking forward to watching the game as always."

Don turned to John's parents.

"Thanks for having me over. Don't forget to give this guy some credit once in a while."

John smiled back at Don.

"I appreciate you stopping by," John said.

As John sat at his desk in his room that night finishing homework, he smiled thinking how fortunate he was to survive this crazy senior year.

"No matter how tomorrow goes, I've been quite fortunate," John said to himself. "Once in a while, life surprises you."

Shortly before 1 p.m. the next day, John stormed onto the court with his 14 teammates to play Lakeside High for the sectional title and trip to state. The Leopards made a one-hour trip to a neutral site and a large gym. John looked around, noticing the packed stands full of North fans. The Lakeside fan section filled up as well, making it a sold-out event.

John focused on his warm-up shots and tried to get as comfortable as he could shooting in the unfamiliar gym. He noticed the two sophomores looked a bit nervous.

"Rob, Deshaun, relax guys, it's just basketball."

"Biggest game of our lives," DeShaun said.

"Don't worry, you may have bigger ones in the next two years. You never know."

"Yeah, I guess."

"Come on, you don't think you'll have a good team in the next couple of years?"

"We should do OK, but this year's team is good."

North got off to a fast start, as Teyshaun and Rashad each hit a three-pointer on their way to a 10-2 lead. As John looked around the gym, he did not see many empty seats in the large gym.

After taking a 20-12 first-quarter lead, North held their lead through most of the next quarter. John wore a look of surprise when Coach Thompson called both him and Juan over to him with two minutes left in the half. John tried to stretch out at the scorer's table next to Juan.

"I haven't been in this early in a while," Juan said. "It's gonna be fun. Two minutes to run and gun."

"Yeah, hopefully we can finish the half strong," John responded.

The two guards entered the game with their team holding a 34-25 lead. John looked up and saw his friends standing and cheering as they took the court. After a few missed shots, the Leopards got the ball on a fast break. John caught Juan's pass and dribbled up to a defender and took a mid-range jumper that rolled off the rim.

"Darn it!" John said to himself as he ran back on defense. After Lakeside hit a three-pointer, North passed the ball around to run some clock, but John saw Joe open in the post and passed the ball inside. Joe took one dribbled and went up strong, putting the ball through the net.

Lakeside rushed the ball down the court and found an open shot but could not hit.

"Let's go!" John yelled to his teammates as they ran the court with 20 seconds left in the half and a 36-28 lead. John saw a one-on-one matchup with Joe in the post once again and made the pass. Joe caught the ball, drawing several defenders away from the perimeter. He kicked the ball out to Juan, who threw a no-look pass to John. After catching the ball, John confidently put up a three-pointer, which swished through the net with the clock winding down. The clock ran out before Lakeside could make another basket, and the North fans shouted their approval of the Leopards' 39-28 halftime lead.

"John's Mr. Instant Offense guys!" DaVonte shouted as the team entered the locker room.

"That's a smooth shot there man," Joe Anthony added.

John smiled, trying to forget the way they treated him the past weeks.

"Fair weather friends, huh?" John said to Rob and DeShaun

sitting next to him.

"Apparently they don't hate you anymore," DeShaun stated.

"My self-worth is determined by whether I can put a ball through a hoop, apparently."

Rob and DeShaun gave him an odd look.

"Just remember, you're not a hotshot when you play well and you're not useless if you don't. Who you are is separate from what kind of ball player you are. These guys wouldn't give me the time of day, and now I hit a couple baskets and they're my friends all of a sudden. It's garbage of course, and you need to recognize it for what it is."

The duo nodded their heads.

"I didn't get it at first. Just make sure you do, 'cause it'll happen to you soon enough. You're good players."

Coach Thompson's speech ended John's admonition, calling on his team to finish strong.

"They have a lot of height on their team, and they're going to try to get it inside in the second half. We need to double on their key guys in the post and close out on shots. This is going to be a battle in the second half, so let's get ready to go."

As the coach talked to specific players about matchups, John thought about Don's comments the previous night. He smiled wondering whether his parents would ever give him their approval.

"Does it even matter?" John asked himself.

"If I do something well, that's its own reward, right?"

John took his warm-up shots for the second half and looked over at the Lakeside side of the court, hoping they could keep the three tall Lakeside players from scoring too many points.

North began the half fast, as the guards displayed their skills against Lakeside's less-accomplished backcourt. The Leopards raced out to 49-30 lead. Coach Thompson sent John and Juan back into the game, but Lakeside went on a run as their forwards began heating up. John felt like Lakeside blitzed them as they scored points on several fast breaks. Their coach quickly sent in several of the starters.

John tried to catch his breath as he took a seat on the bench.

"That was rough," John said, sliding into a seat next to the two sophomores. "We need to do a better job getting back on defense."

The third quarter ended with North holding onto a 51-46 lead. Coach Thompson's face turned red as he shouted instructions to his players.

"His face now matches the color of his tie," John joked to those around him.

"He'd start yelling at you if he heard that," Erick Samuels said.

"Oh, I forgot, this is serious business. No smiles allowed during a game."

The team began to settle down once again as a couple of jump shots from the guards put the Leopards comfortably ahead for the moment. Midway through the third, Coach Thompson called John and Juan over to him.

"You're both going to be in for a couple minutes to give the guards a breather. I'm giving our forwards a rest one at a time. Braden's out now, but he'll go in with you. Let's keep the lead."

John nodded as the buzzer sounded, giving them a chance to get in the game. The game seemed to slow down for him as the two teams tried to score points in the post. Terrance White hit a couple of jump shots to give the Leopards a 59-50 advantage with four minutes left in the game. As promised, Coach Thompson pulled John and three others in order to get all five starters back in the game.

Teammates congratulated everyone as they found a seat on

the bench. Both teams traded baskets on the next few possessions, but Lakeside began fouling in order to extend the game with a minute and a half left with the score 65-56.

"I think we might have this one," John said with a smile to his bench mates.

"Don't jinx it," Juan added.

After a couple missed three-pointers, Lakeside called off the dogs and decided not to foul, trailing 68-58 with under a minute to go. Coach Thompson waved for seniors John and Darnell Jackson to the scorer's table, along with the three players who had not seen action, including Erick Samuels, Rob and DeShaun.

"You're getting some action in a sectional final game, how cool is that?" John said to the sophomores.

"And we're winning it, which is the best thing," Rob added.

Once in the game, Lakeside called a timeout to get their reserve players in for the final 30 seconds. Juan inbounded the ball to John, who dribbled past half court. Lakeside tried to trap him, but John broke through between the two players as the ref blew the whistle for a foul. John went to the line as the crowd cheered. John sunk both free throws and gave a smile to his friends in the stands on the way down the court.

A Lakeside guard tossed up a three-pointer that missed badly, and the rebound found its way to John. He looked up and saw DeShaun streaking down the court. John heaved the ball toward the basket, as DeShaun caught the ball in stride and made a layup as the final seconds ran off the clock for a 73-58 win. The team crashed into each other in a mid-court pile to celebrate.

"State-bound!" Juan yelled as joined the pile.

John eventually found his way to his friends and family after the medal ceremony.

Amber and Courtney gave him high-fives as they walked

onto the court. Amber looked at him, questioningly.

"So, you get in a fight, get kicked off the team, deal with a bully and then go to state, huh?"

John grinned. "Not how I would have drawn it up, but hey, sometimes things have a way of working out."

About the Author

Author Peter Spicer works as a high school para professional and resides in Waunakee, WI with his wife, Jessica, and son. This is his first novel but conducted years of "research" for the book as a frequent "member of the board" in high school and college. Spicer's love of sports led him to play high school football, basketball and baseball, and college football and baseball, including a year of semi-professional football. He worked as a reporter for over five years at several Wisconsin weekly newspapers, covering sports and local news. Spicer has a bachelor's degree in Humanities with a minor in writing. In 2016, he earned a Master of Liberal Arts from Texas Christian University in Fort Worth, TX. In Spicer's free time, he enjoys playing basketball, working out and playing the French horn. He also follows his favorite professional and college sports teams, some of which leave him bitterly disappointed.